Harlequin Romance® presents...

LUCY GORDON

Readers all over the world love Lucy Gordon for powerful emotional drama, spine-tingling intensity and Italian heroes! Her storytelling talent has won her countless awards, including two RITA® Awards!

Praise for Lucy Gordon:

"Gordon's characters are so lifelike, they dance across the page and the story is so emotionally deep that one feels like a participant and not an observer."
—*www.romantictimes.com*

"In *The Wedding Arrangement*, Lucy Gordon blends fantastic characters, tender romance, emotional intensity, powerful drama and witty dialogue in an unforgettable story which you will not be able to put down."
—*www.cataromance.com*

"You have to trust me," Matteo said. "I know that your experience has left you wary, but if you don't trust me, what will you do?"

"I don't know," Holly whispered.

Something in her rebelled at this situation. Inch by inch she was being drawn under his control and she would fight that to her last breath.

"I don't know," she cried.

Matteo took hold of her. His hands were hard and warm, reassuring even as they commanded.

"Trust me," he said softly. "You do, don't you? Tell me that you trust me. *Say it.*"

"Yes," she whispered. She hardly knew she was saying the words. Something stronger than herself had taken her over, and it was no use fighting. She felt hypnotized.

LUCY GORDON

One Summer in Italy...

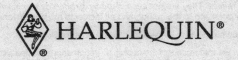

HARLEQUIN®

TORONTO • NEW YORK • LONDON
AMSTERDAM • PARIS • SYDNEY • HAMBURG
STOCKHOLM • ATHENS • TOKYO • MILAN • MADRID
PRAGUE • WARSAW • BUDAPEST • AUCKLAND

ISBN-13: 978-0-373-03933-3
ISBN-10:   0-373-03933-6

ONE SUMMER IN ITALY...

First North American Publication 2007.

Copyright © 2006 by Lucy Gordon.

This edition published by arrangement with Harlequin Books S.A.

® and TM are trademarks of the publisher. Trademarks indicated with
® are registered in the United States Patent and Trademark Office, the
Canadian Trade Marks Office and in other countries.

www.eHarlequin.com

Printed in U.S.A.

Lucy Gordon cut her writing teeth on magazine journalism, interviewing many of the world's most interesting men, including Warren Beatty, Richard Chamberlain, Roger Moore, Sir Alec Guinness and Sir John Gielgud. She also camped out with lions in Africa, and had many other unusual experiences that have often provided the background for her books. She is married to a Venetian, whom she met while on holiday in Venice. They got engaged within two days.

Two of her books have won the Romance Writers of America RITA® Award: *Song of the Lorelei* in 1990 and *His Brother's Child* in 1998 for the Best Traditional Romance category.

You can visit her Web site at www.lucy-gordon.com

Let Lucy Gordon sweep you away to beautiful Rome, a truly romantic city, in her breathtaking story…

Soak up the atmosphere of this truly remarkable setting, and indulge your senses. Wend your way through pretty cobbled streets, and feel the history of the city seep into your bones as you pass the stunning Colosseum, Pantheon, the ancient forum and Palatine Hill. Be amazed when you enter the stunning walled Vatican City with its magnificent art treasures and the spectacular St. Peter's Cathedral. Later on, relax in an outdoor café on a bustling *piazza* with your delicious, creamy gelato, or rich Italian coffee.

When the sun goes down the city comes alive. Wander past the illuminated fountains and monuments on your way to a *trattoria* and enjoy mouthwatering Roman delicacies, sip fine wine or *prosecco* and finish the evening off with a romantic stroll along the banks of the River Tiber.

Experience all this and more in
One Summer in Italy…

CHAPTER ONE

NOT much longer—if I can just hold out—please, please, don't let them catch me...

The soft vibration of the speeding train seemed to be part of her thoughts. It was five minutes late but she should still reach Rome in time to get to the airport and catch her plane home.

Just a hundred miles to Rome—that's not much really—unless the police saw me get on this train...

Had anyone seen her? She'd hurried, keeping her head down, trying to get lost in the crowd. Nobody had troubled her so far, but it was too soon to feel safe.

Perhaps she would never feel truly safe again. The man she had loved and trusted had betrayed her, throwing her to the wolves to save his own skin. Even if she managed to keep her freedom, the world had changed, becoming ugly and bitter, like the inside of her own mind.

Somebody eased past her in the corridor and she turned hastily away, staring out of the window to conceal her face. Outside, the Italian countryside, bathed in the glowing colours of summer, rushed by, but she was barely aware of its beauty. Only her fear existed.

When she next looked, she could see two uniformed men at the end of the corridor.

Police!

She must escape before they reached her.

Edge away slowly. Don't attract attention. Try to look casual.

She wondered exactly what kind of description of her they had: Name, Sarah Conroy, but answers only to Holly; a young woman in her late twenties, tall, perhaps a little too slim, with light brown hair, cut short, blue eyes and a face with nothing special about it: a face that hadn't lived very much.

Nondescript. Yes, that was the word for her, and for the first time she was glad. It might save her now.

Here was the end of the carriage. A short step and she was in the next one. It was first class, divided into compartments. But each one had the blinds down and it was too risky to take shelter in one of them without some idea of what she would find.

Without warning, the blind beside her flew up and she found herself staring straight at a little girl. She was about eight years old and in a childish temper. That was all Holly had time to take in before making a lightning decision.

It took a split-second to open the door, dart inside and pull the blind down again.

In the corner a young woman looked up from her book and opened her mouth, but Holly just managed to get in first.

'Please don't make a sound. I need your help desperately.'

She realised too late that she was speaking English. They wouldn't understand a word. But before she could call on her unreliable Italian the child broke in speaking English.

'Good afternoon, *signorina*,' she said with quaint formality, 'I am very happy to meet you.'

Her temper had vanished as if by magic. She was smiling as, with perfect self-possession, she offered one small hand. Dazed, Holly took it in her own.

'How—how do you do?' she murmured mechanically.

'I am very well, thank you,' the child responded carefully. 'My name is Liza Fallucci. What is your name, please?'

'Holly,' she said slowly, trying to understand what was happening.

'Are you English?'

'Yes, I am English.'

'I am very glad you are English.'

She was beaming as though she really was glad, as if someone had given her a big, beautiful gift.

The train slowed suddenly and the child nearly fell. The young woman put out a hand to steady her.

'Careful, *piccina*. You're still not steady on your feet.'

Now Holly saw clearly what she had missed before. The little girl was unable to walk properly. One leg was encased in a support, and as she moved she reached out to hold on to the seats.

'I'm all right, Berta,' she insisted.

Berta smiled. 'You always say that, but you want to do too much too soon. I'm here to help you.'

'I don't want to be helped,' Liza told her stubbornly.

She tried to haul herself up onto a seat, but slithered off and was only saved from falling by Holly's hand. Instead of throwing it off, Liza used it to steady herself, and even allowed Holly to assist her as she wriggled to safety.

Berta gave a wry grimace, but the child's snub did not seem to trouble her. She was in her twenties, robustly built with a cheerful, good-natured face.

'I'm sorry,' Holly began to say.

'Is all right,' Berta assured her in careful English. 'The *piccina* is often cross with me, but—she hates to be an invalid. I am her nurse.'

'I don't need a nurse,' Liza insisted. 'I'm well now.'

Her chin set mulishly, and even in her agitation Holly knew

a flash of amusement. This little one had a will of her own. But for the moment she was a lifeline.

Berta began to protest. '*Forse, ma—*'

'Berta, why do you speak Italian?' Liza demanded. 'This lady is English and she doesn't understand you.'

'I understand some Italian,' Holly began to say, but Liza interrupted her too.

'No, no, the English never understand foreign languages,' she declared imperiously. 'We will speak English.' She scowled at Berta, evidently commanding her to keep quiet.

'How do you know English people are no use at foreign languages?' Holly asked.

'My *Mamma* told me so. She was English and she could speak Italian but only because she'd been here for so long. She and Poppa spoke both languages.'

'That must be why your English is so good.'

Liza beamed.

'Mamma and I used to speak it all the time.'

'Used to?'

'The *Signora* dead,' Berta said softly.

Liza did not reply to this in words, but Holly felt the sudden tightening of the little hand on hers, and she squeezed back.

After a moment, Liza said, 'She promised to take me to England. I mean to go one day.'

'I think you'll like it,' Holly assured her.

'Tell me about England. What is it like? Is it very big?'

'About the same size as Italy.'

'Do you know Portsmouth?'

'A little. It's on the south coast and I come from the Midlands.'

'But you do know it?' Liza persisted eagerly.

'I've spent some time there.'

'Did you see the boats?'

'Yes, and I went sailing,' Holly replied.

'Mamma lived in Portsmouth. She liked sailing. She said it was the loveliest feeling in the world.'

'It is. Having the wind in your face, feeling the boat move under you—'

'Tell me,' Liza begged. 'Tell me all about it.'

It was hard to speak light-heartedly when she was full of dread, and her mind was on whatever was happening further down the train. But she forced herself to do it. It was her only chance, yet it was more than that. The child's shining eyes showed that this meant the world to her, and Holly was swept by a sudden determination to give her whatever happiness she could.

Her memories were vague but she embellished them, inventing where she had to, trying to bolster the illusion that the little girl wanted. She had found someone who reminded her, however tenuously, of her dead mother and happier times. Not for anything would Holly have spoiled it for her.

Now and then Liza would interrupt, asking about a new word, and practising until she was sure she had it. She was a quick learner and never needed to be told twice.

Suddenly Berta began to grow agitated, looking at the door. Seeing her, Holly too began to worry.

'I was just wondering when the judge would be returning,' Berta said.

Holly grew tense. 'Judge?' she asked.

'Liza's father is Judge Matteo Fallucci. He is visiting a friend in another compartment. I thought he—' she struggled for the words '—perhaps—return by now. I can't wait. I need,' she dropped her voice to a modest whisper, '*gabinetto*.'

'Yes, but—'

'You will stay with the *piccina per un momento, si? Grazie.*'

She rushed out as she spoke, leaving Holly no option but to stay.

She began to feel desperate. How long would she be trapped here? She had hoped to be safe, but it seemed she'd jumped out of the frying-pan, into the fire.

'You will stay?' Liza echoed.

'Just for a moment—'

'No, stay for always.'

'I wish I could, I really do, but I have to go. When Berta comes back—'

'I hope she never comes back,' Liza said sulkily.

'Why? Is she unkind to you?'

'No, she means to be kind, but...' Liza gave an eloquent shrug. 'I can't talk to her. She doesn't understand. She thinks if I eat my food and do my exercises—that's all there is. If I try to talk about...about things, she just stares.'

That had been Holly's impression of Berta too; well-meaning but unsubtle. It hadn't seemed to occur to her that she should not have left the child with a stranger, even for a moment.

But perhaps she'd hurried and, even now, was on her way back. Meaning just to take a quick look, Holly turned to the door and ran straight into the man standing there.

She hadn't heard him enter, and didn't know how long he'd been there. She collided with him before she saw him, and had an instant impression of a hard, unyielding body towering over her.

'Who are you?' he demanded sharply in Italian. 'What are you doing here?'

'*Signore*—' Suddenly she couldn't breathe.

'Who are you?' he said again in a harsh voice.

It was Liza who came to her rescue, limping forward and saying hurriedly, 'No, Poppa, the *signorina* is English, so we only speak English.' She took Holly's hand, saying firmly, 'She comes from Portsmouth, like Mamma. And she's my friend.'

A change came over him. With an odd feeling, Holly remembered how Liza, too, had changed. She had become joyful, while this man seemed to flinch. Yet they were reacting to the same thing. It was a mystery.

Liza drew her back to the seat, keeping hold of her hand as if to say that her new friend was under her protection. Even though she was so young, her strength of will was clear. She had probably inherited it from her father, Holly thought.

He eyed Holly coldly.

'You turn up in my compartment, and I'm expected to accept your presence with equanimity?'

'I'm—just an English tourist,' she said carefully.

'I think I begin to understand. There's a commotion further down the train. But I imagine you know that.'

She faced him. 'Yes, I do know.'

'And no doubt it has something to do with your sudden appearance here. No, don't answer. I can make up my own mind.'

'Then let me go,' Holly said.

'Go where?'

His tone was implacable. And so was everything else about him, she realised. Tall, lean, hard, with dark, slightly sunken eyes that glared over a prominent nose, he looked every inch a judge: the kind of man who would lay down the law and expect to be obeyed in life as well as in court.

She searched his face, trying to detect in it something yielding, but she could find no hope. She tried to rise.

'Sit down,' he told her. 'If you go out of that door you'll run straight into the arms of the police, who are examining everyone's passports.'

She sank back in her seat. This was the end.

'Are you a suspicious person?' he asked. 'Is that why Berta has vanished?'

Liza giggled. 'No, Berta has gone along the corridor for a few minutes.'

'She asked me to look after your daughter while she was away,' Holly said. 'But now you're here—'

'Stay where you are,' he ordered.

She had half risen in her seat, but his tone of command was so final that she had no choice but to fall back.

'Are you really running away from the police?' Liza asked her. 'How exciting!'

Her father closed his eyes.

'Is it too much to hope that you'll remember I am a judge?' he asked.

'Oh, but that doesn't matter, Poppa,' the child said blithely. 'Holly needs our help.'

'Liza—'

The child scrambled painfully out of her seat and stood in front of him, taking his outstretched hand for support and regarding him with a challenging look.

'She's my friend, Poppa.'

'Your friend? And you've known her for how long?'

'Ten minutes.'

'Well, then—'

'But who cares?' Liza demanded earnestly. 'It doesn't matter how long you've known someone. You used to say that.'

'I don't think I actually said—'

'You did, you did.' Liza's voice rose as she began to be upset. 'You said, with some people you knew at once that they were going to be terribly important to you. You and Mamma—'

Without warning she burst into tears, drowning out the rest of her words.

Holly waited for him to reach out and hug his child, but something seemed to have happened to him. His face had acquired a grey tinge and was suddenly set in forbidding lines, as though the mention of his dead wife had murdered something inside him. It was like watching a man being turned into a tombstone.

Liza's tears had turned into violent sobs, yet still he did not embrace her. Unable to bear it any longer, Holly scooped her up so that the little girl was sitting in her lap, her face buried against her.

At that moment the door of the compartment slid back. Holly drew in a sharp breath as the full horror of her position crashed over her. The police were coming in. And she was in the hands of a judge. Now there was no hope.

A man in a police uniform entered, and immediately froze at the sight of the judge, whom he clearly recognised. He spoke in Italian, which Holly just managed to follow.

'Signor Fallucci, forgive me, I did not know—a small matter.'

'What is this small matter?' The judge sounded as though speaking was suddenly an effort.

'We are searching for a woman who, we have reason to believe, is on this train. Her name is Sarah Conroy.'

He was forced to raise his voice to be heard above Liza's sobbing, and turned to Holly.

'*Signorina,* is your name—?'

But before he could complete the question Liza raised her head. Her face was red and tears streamed down her face as she cried,

'Her name is Holly and she's my friend. *Go away!*'

'I only—'

'She's Holly,' Liza screamed. 'And she's mine, she's *mine*!'

'Hush,' Holly whispered. 'Hold on to me.'

Liza was already clinging around her throat with arms so tight that Holly was almost choking. She stayed holding the little girl, offering what comfort she could.

If she'd been thinking clearly she would have realised that Liza was obscuring her face from the policeman, and her noisy sobs were covering any suspicious Englishness in Holly's voice. But right now she was beyond understanding. She cared only for Liza's shattering grief and whatever she could do to ease it.

So she gathered her in an even tighter embrace, murmuring words of comfort and tenderness until the sobbing little girl in her arms grew less tense.

The judge had seemed almost in a trance, but now he roused himself with an effort.

'I think you should go now,' he said. 'My daughter is not well, and it isn't good for her to be upset.'

By now the young policeman had noticed the wheelchair and the supports on Liza's legs. He nodded to show his understanding.

'I'll leave you in peace. Forgive me. Good day, *signore, signorina.*'

He couldn't get out fast enough.

For a while they travelled in silence. Holly met the judge's eyes, trying to read them, but found them cool and impenetrable.

'Why did you do that?' she asked.

He glanced at his little daughter, as if to say she was answer enough. Which was true, Holly thought. He had had no choice, and yet—

'Would you have preferred the alternative?' he asked.

'Of course not, but you don't know me—'

'That will be remedied when I'm ready.'

'But—'

LUCY GORDON   17

'It will be best if you say no more,' he replied in a voice that brooked no argument. 'We shall soon be in Rome, and later I will tell you as much as you need to know.'

'But when we get to Rome I shall be leaving—'

'I think not,' he said in a tone of finality.

'Is Holly coming home with us?' Liza asked, smiling at the prospect.

'Of course,' he told her.

'But—my plane—' Holly tried to say.

This time he did not answer in words, but the flicker of his eyes was enough to inform her that he, not she, was calling the shots.

Liza showed her happiness by twining her hand in Holly's and beaming at her father.

'Thank you, Poppa,' she said, as though he had just bought her a precious gift.

The compartment door slid back and Berta entered, looking nervous at the sight of her employer.

'You should not have left Liza alone,' he growled.

'*Scusi, signore*—but she was not alone.'

The judge seemed disposed to argue, but then he looked at his little daughter, snuggling happily in Holly's arms, and the sight seemed to strike him silent.

Now that Liza had secured her object her tears dried like magic.

'You'll like our house,' she told Holly. 'I'll show you all over the gardens and…'

She chattered on and Holly tried to keep up with her, putting in the odd word, although her mind was whirling. While she smiled at Liza she was intensely aware of the man in the opposite seat, watching her with sharp, appraising eyes.

He was sizing her up, she guessed, mentally taking notes,

trying to come to a decision. In other words, he was behaving like a judge deciding the verdict, with the sentence to follow.

He might have been in his late thirties, although his stern face and haughty demeanour made him seem older. He was handsome in a fierce, uncompromising way that had more to do with something in his eyes than with the shape of his features.

Suddenly he spoke, indicating the small bag that hung from her shoulder. 'What do you have in there?'

'My passport,' she said, 'and papers generally.'

'Let me see.'

She handed him the bag and he glanced through briefly, examining the papers until he came to her passport. Without hesitation he took it, placing it in an inside pocket of his jacket.

Holly opened her mouth to protest but was checked by his glance. It was hard, forbidding, and it compelled her silence.

'Good,' he said, handing the bag to her. 'You have all you need.'

'I need my passport.'

'No, you don't. Do it my way and don't argue.'

'Now, look—'

'Do you want my help or don't you?'

'Of course, but I—'

'Then take my advice and stay as quiet as you can. From now on, not a word. Try to look stupid. Practise that if you have to, but don't speak.'

'But I had to leave a suitcase further down the train,' she burst out. 'I must get it.'

'Why?'

'My clothes—'

'You don't need them. And trying to recover your possessions would lead you into danger.'

Into the arms of the police, he meant, and she realised he

was right. Holly would have been grateful for his warning but for a feeling he was chiefly concerned about the inconvenience to himself.

The train was slowing, gliding into Rome railway station, coming to a halt. Immediately a man appeared wearing the uniform of a chauffeur and signalled through the window. The judge signalled back, and a moment later the man entered the compartment.

'The car is waiting, *signore*,' he said, bestowing only the briefest glance on Holly.

Liza immediately put her hand in Holly's and stood up.

'I think you should use the wheelchair,' her father said.

Liza thrust out her lower lip and shook her head. 'I want to go with you,' she said, looking up at Holly.

'Then I'll take you,' she said. 'But I think you should go in the wheelchair.'

'All right,' Liza said, docile as long as she had what she wanted.

The platform was the last on the station. Beside it was a wall, with a large archway almost opposite their carriage. It took only a few moments to leave the train and move beneath the arch to where a limousine was waiting. Liza sat contentedly in the wheelchair while Holly pushed her, praying that this would give her an extra disguise against any police eyes that were watching.

At the car door the chauffeur took the chair and packed it into the trunk. The judge got into the front, while Holly and Berta sat in the back with Liza between them.

Holly tried to believe that this was really happening. Even the noiseless, gliding movement of the car, as it left the station, couldn't quite convince her.

A moveable glass screen divided the front from the back of the car, and the judge pulled this firmly across, shutting them off from each other. Holly saw him take out a mobile phone and speak into it, but she couldn't hear the words.

They turned south and sped smoothly on until the crowded city fell away behind them, the road turned to cobblestones and monuments began to appear along the way.

'They're ancient tombs and this is the Via Appia Antica,' Liza told her. 'We live further down.'

About half a mile further on they turned through a high stone arch and began the journey along a winding, tree-lined road. The foliage of high summer was at its most magnificent, so the house came into view piece by piece, and it wasn't until the last moment that Holly saw its full glory.

It was a mansion, obviously several hundred years old, made from honey-coloured stone.

As the car stopped a middle-aged woman emerged, making for the rear door, to open it, while the chauffeur opened the front door for the judge.

'Good evening, Anna,' the judge said briefly. 'Is everything ready for our guest?'

'Yes, *signore*,' the housekeeper said respectfully. 'I personally attended to the *signorina's* room.'

So she was expected, Holly thought, remembering the phone call in the car. This and the smoothly efficient movements of the servants increased her sense of well-oiled wheels, which might be conveying her away from danger, but would roll over her just as easily.

He had called her his guest, but the judge did not welcome her as one. It was Liza who took her hand, drawing her into the house and displaying her home with pride. Inside the hall there were more servants, all giving her the controlled curious glances of people who had been warned ahead of time, then hastily looking away.

'I will take the *signorina* to her room,' Anna said. 'Follow me, please.'

The way led up a grand staircase that curved to the next floor, ending in luxurious marble tiles on which her heels echoed up to the door of her room.

The room itself was startling, with a marble floor and an exposed stone wall that gave it an air of rustic charm without lessening its elegance. Two floor-length windows flooded the room with light. The bed, which was large enough to sleep three, was a four-poster, hung with ivory net curtains.

The rest of the furniture was in dark wood with a rich sheen, and ornately carved. To Holly's eye the items had the look of valuable antiques. She had reason to know this, having recently received a terrifying education in antiques.

'Are you sure this is the right room?' she asked, overwhelmed.

'Signor Fallucci insisted on the very best guest room,' Anna replied. 'He says that every attention must be paid to you.'

'That's very kind of him,' she murmured.

'If you will follow me, *signorina*…'

Anna showed her through a door to a bathroom with walls also of exposed stone, an antique marble basin and hand-painted tiles. Thick ivory towels hung on the walls.

'If the *signorina* is satisfied—'

'Yes, it's lovely,' Holly said mechanically. She could feel a net closing about her.

'If you would care to rest now, a meal will be sent to you here.'

When she was alone she sat down on the bed, feeling winded. On the face of it she'd fallen on her feet, but that wasn't how it felt. The more she was welcomed and pampered, the more unnatural it all seemed, and the more nervous she became.

Everything made it clear to her that Judge Fallucci was a

supremely powerful as well as a wealthy man. He was using both to prepare a niche for her, so comfortable that she wouldn't want to leave.

But the fact was that she could not leave, even if she wanted to. He'd taken her passport; she had little money and no clothes. Now she had to depend on this stranger, who had seized control of her for his own purposes.

Despite the luxurious surface of her surroundings, she was a helpless prisoner.

CHAPTER TWO

SUPPER, when it arrived, was a feast for the gods. Soup made with ray fish and broccoli, lamb roasted in a sauce of garlic, rosemary, vinegar and anchovy, followed by *tozzetti*, sweet cookies made from sugar, almonds and aniseed.

With every course came the proper wine, rough red, crisp white or icy mineral water. Everything was perfect. Nothing had been left to chance.

When she had finished eating Holly went to the window and watched the last rays of the sun setting over the garden, which stretched out of sight, a maze of pines, Cyprus trees and flowers, threaded by paths, along which a tall man was strolling.

'Signor Fallucci walks there every evening,' Anna said, just behind her. She had come into the room to collect the tray. 'Always he goes to visit his wife's grave.'

'She's buried here?'

'In a patch of ground that was specially consecrated.'

'How long has he been a widower?'

'Eight months. She died in a train crash, last December, and the little girl was badly hurt.'

'Poor little mite.'

'You can just see the monument, there—where the setting sun just touches the tip. Every evening he stands before it for a long time. When it's dark he walks back to the house, but here there is only more darkness for him.'

'I can imagine,' she breathed.

'He says he will see you in his study in twenty minutes,' Anna added, departing with the tray.

Earlier, the high-handed message would have annoyed her. Now, watching him moving in the dusk, she realised that there had been a subtle change. He looked lonely, almost crushed. She began to feel a little more confident. Perhaps he wasn't so fearsome after all.

At the exact time she knocked on the study door, and received a cool, *'Avanti!'*

Entering, she found herself in a room, dominated by a large oak desk, with a table lamp that provided the room's only light. Outside its arc she was dimly aware of walls lined with leather-bound books.

He was standing by the window, looking out, and turned when she entered. But he didn't move out of the shadows, and she couldn't make out much more than his outline.

'Good evening, *signorina*.' His voice seemed to come from a distance. 'You would prefer that we talk in English?'

'Yes, thank you, Signor Fallucci.'

'Your room is to your liking?'

'Yes, and the meal was delicious.'

'Of course.' His tone suggested this was the natural order of things. 'Otherwise my staff would have heard my displeasure. Would you care to sit down?'

He indicated the chair facing the desk. It was a command, not a request, and she sat.

'I know something about you from my daughter,' he said, seating himself opposite her. 'Your name is Holly, you are English and you come from Portsmouth.'

'No, I don't.'

'Didn't you tell Liza that you lived in Portsmouth?' he said sharply. 'She thinks you did.'

'That's a mistake, and I'll explain if you'll let me finish.' For all her resolution to tread carefully she couldn't keep an annoyed edge out of her voice. She was damned if she'd let him cross-examine her as though they were in court.

He leaned back in his chair and made a gesture that meant, 'Go on.'

'I come from a little town in the English Midlands. Portsmouth is down on the south coast and I know it quite well because I've spent some holidays there. I tried to tell Liza that, but the place means a lot to her because of her mother. So I talked about it, as much as I could remember, and I think she seized on that, built on it and just blotted out the bit she didn't need. She's clinging on to something that can bring her a scrap of comfort. Children do it all the time.'

'And not just children,' he murmured.

There was a silence.

'Please go on,' he said at last.

'I don't know what else there is to say.'

He'd been half-turned away from her. Now he swung around and spoke in a hard voice.

'We have a difficult situation. I'm a judge and you are on the run from the police.'

'You don't know that,' she challenged. 'They didn't identify me in the compartment today.'

'Very shrewd. Clearly they know little about the woman they are seeking, not even that she goes by the name of Holly—whatever her real name may be.'

He was silent, watching her. When she didn't speak he

shrugged and said, 'You could, of course, give me any name you like.'

'Not while you're holding my passport,' she replied.

He nodded and a glimmer of a smile flickered over his face.

'You were trying to trip me up,' she said furiously.

'If I was, I didn't succeed. Good.'

'And if I had succeeded?'

'Then I'd have been disappointed in you. As it is, you present me with a problem.'

'You could have solved it in a moment this afternoon.'

'That would have been impossible,' he said heavily. 'You know why.'

'Liza. Yes, you couldn't have done that to that poor little girl.'

'And it's left me in a very awkward position,' he said, half angrily.

'But you didn't actually tell the police any lies.'

'I can't console myself with such nit-picking.'

'So now you want to know all about me, and what I'm supposed to have done,' she said, bracing herself.

His reply astonished her.

'At this moment, the very last thing I want is to know *all* about you. I know that you are a decent person, incapable of evil.'

'How can you know that?'

'Because I've met a thousand criminals and I know the difference. You develop an instinct. My instinct tells me that at worst you involved yourself in some foolishness that you didn't understand. And also,' his voice slowed and he added reluctantly, 'also because of the way Liza clung to you. That little girl's instinct is even surer than mine. If you had a criminal heart she would never have turned to you and wept in your arms.'

Holly was silent, amazed. She would not have expected such insight from this man.

Suddenly he rounded on her. 'Am I wrong?' he asked sharply.

'No,' she said. 'You're not wrong.'

'Good. Then I need to know a little about you, but let's keep it to the minimum. Give me a rough idea, but no details and no names.'

'It was as you said. I got caught up in something bad, not realising what was really happening. When I discovered the truth I ran, fast.'

'How old are you?'

'Twenty-eight.'

'Who knows you're in Italy?'

'Nobody. I have no family.'

'What about your work colleagues?'

'None. I'm not in work just now.'

'There must be *someone* in England who'll think it strange if you don't return by a certain date.'

'There isn't. I live alone in a small rented house. I didn't know how long I'd be away, so I told my neighbour to expect me when she saw me. I could vanish off the face of the earth and it would be ages before anyone noticed.'

She said the last words in a tone of discovery, as it was borne in on her how completely isolated she was. It was something she had vaguely recognised, but it was only now that the reality was brought home to her.

And if I'd had my wits about me, she told herself, I wouldn't have admitted it to him. Now he knows how totally I'm in his power.

In the silence she could sense him surveying her, probably thinking how dull and unsophisticated she was for her age. It was true. She knew nothing, and it had left her vulnerable to Bruno Vanelli. Vulnerable in her heart and her life, in ways that she was only now beginning to understand.

When she'd met Bruno she'd been mostly ignorant of the world and men, and he had guessed that and played her like a fool.

Which was what I was, she thought bitterly. A fool.

'Tell me about that suitcase you were so anxious to recover,' the judge said. 'Is there anything incriminating in it?'

'No, I just didn't like losing my clothes.'

'Anything there that can identify you?'

'Nothing.'

'How can you be sure?'

'Because of Uncle Josh.'

'*Uncle Josh*? He's travelling with you?'

'No, of course not. He's dead.'

'He's dead but he tells you what to pack?' he recited in a voice that strongly suggested he was dealing with a lunatic.

'I know it sounds batty, but it's the truth,' she explained.

'Batty? You'll have to excuse me. I'm discovering unexpected holes in my English.'

'It means crazy, weird. I feel a bit weird. In fact, very weird.'

His answer was to fill a glass and put it into her hand. It turned out to be brandy.

'Give yourself a moment to calm down,' he said in a gentler voice. 'Then tell me about Uncle Josh and how he directs your packing from his grave.'

There was a slight quirk to his mouth that might almost have been humour.

'Years ago,' she said, 'he went on holiday and on the journey someone stole his suitcase. There were some papers in it that contained his address. When he got home he found his house ransacked.

'Since then none of my family have ever packed anything that could identify us. Papers have to go in a bag that you keep on you. It's an article of faith. You swear allegiance to your country and you vow not to leave bits of paper in suitcases.'

Holly choked suddenly as the sheer idiocy of this conversation came over her. Now nothing mattered but a wild desire for maniacal laughter. She controlled it as long as she could, but then her resistance collapsed and she shook.

The judge rose quickly, rescuing her glass and setting it down out of danger.

'I suppose this was inevitable,' he said. 'If you're going to have hysterics you'd better have them and get it over with.'

She jumped up and turned away from him, unwilling to let him see how vulnerable she felt at this moment.

'I am not having hysterics,' she said firmly. 'I just—don't know what's happening.'

'Then why are you shaking?' he said, moving behind her and placing his hands on her arms.

'I'm—I'm not—I'm—'

He drew her slowly back against him and folded his arms across her in the front. It wasn't a hug, because he didn't turn her to face him. He was as impersonal as a man could be who actually had his arms about a woman. Even through the whirling in her head she knew that he was soothing her in a way that involved no suspicion of intimacy.

It was oddly reassuring. He was telling her silently that she was safe with him because there was a line he would not cross, while the warmth and power of the body behind her seemed to infuse her with new strength.

'Are you all right?' he asked quietly.

His breath fluttered heatedly against the back of her neck. She tried to ignore it, as she guessed he expected her to do. In fact, she doubted if he'd given the matter a thought.

'I don't know. I don't even know who I am any more.'

'That's probably the safest option for you,' he observed with a touch of wryness.

Releasing her, he guided her back to where she could sit down, and said almost casually, 'I suppose it was a man who lured you into this?'

'Yes, I suppose it's that obvious. He gave me a line and I fell for it. I don't know exactly what happened. Maybe they caught him and he managed to put the blame on me.'

'My love, trust me—love me. Nothing matters except that we should be together.'

'Saving himself by sacrificing you?'

'Yes, I think he must have done that.'

'How refreshing to find you so realistic.'

'After what's happened to me, I have no choice but to be realistic.'

His mouth twisted ironically.

'Some are born realistic,' he misquoted. 'Some achieve realism, and some have it thrust upon them.'

'Nobody is born realistic,' she parried. 'We all have it thrust upon us, in one way or another.'

'How true! How bitterly true.'

He spoke so softly that she wasn't sure she'd really heard, and when she regarded him with a questioning look he walked away to the window. He stayed there, not speaking, for several minutes. At last he said over his shoulder, 'I dare say Anna has spoken to you of my wife.'

'She did say that Signora Fallucci died in a train accident, and that Liza was also injured. Liza herself told me that her mother was English. I felt that she seized on me for that reason.'

'You're right. It struck me as soon as I entered the compartment. I saw something in Liza's face that I haven't seen for months. She was content, almost happy. And then, the way she clung to you—I suppose I made my decision then.'

'The decision to take me over, lock, stock and barrel? The decision to acquire me at whatever cost, even if it meant out-bidding the police?'

'That's a cynical way of putting it.'

'How else would you put it?'

'I might say that you were in need of help, as am I, and we decided to assist each other.'

'When did I *decide* anything?'

'My dear *signorina*, forgive me if I have been too precipi-tate. Clearly I should have introduced you to the police and waited while you chose between us.'

Silence!

He was smiling, but behind the smile there was the steel of a man used to having his own way and determined that it was going to continue. He had her helpless, and he knew it.

'In fact, neither of us made the decision,' he said with a shrug. 'Liza made it. I'm merely following her wishes. I admit that the circumstances aren't ideal but I didn't create them. I had to act quickly.'

It was true, and every instinct warned her to go carefully and not antagonise him. But too many years of going care-fully rose up in defiance now, robbing her of caution.

'No, you didn't create them, but you knew how to take ad-vantage of them, didn't you? Despite your talk of following Liza's wishes, I'm little better than a prisoner—'

'Not at all. Walk out whenever you like.'

'You know I can't. I have no clothes, no money, no passport...'

His response was to reach into his jacket and hand her a fistful of notes.

'Go,' he said. 'I will order that the doors are opened for you.'

She backed away from him, refusing to touch the money and saying wildly, 'Oh, yes? Where am I? Where do I go? What do I do? You're just playing with me, and you should be ashamed.'

Holly could tell she'd taken him by surprise. There was a flash of anger, then he nodded.

'I admire your courage, *signorina*. Foolhardy but admirable.'

'Perhaps it is you who is being foolhardly,' she snapped, not appeased. 'You took me into your house, and all you know about me is that I'm on the run.'

'But you've assured me that you're innocent.'

'Well, I would say that, wouldn't I?' she hurled at him. 'It was a pack of lies to protect myself. How would you know the difference?'

'*Maria vergine!* If you imagine that you could deceive me for a moment, you're mistaken. If I didn't think your worst fault was incredible naivety I would never allow you near my daughter.'

Her antagonism died. He'd read her correctly. Naivety was the kindest word for her.

'Now, can we stop fencing and start being practical?' he continued. 'I want you to stay here as a companion to Liza. Berta does an excellent job caring for her, but she can't give her what she really needs, the thing that only you can give her.

'It's clear that she sees you as a connection with her mother. You're English, you can speak the language with her as her *mamma* did, and that will comfort her until she's ready to let go. If you can do that, there may be something I can do for you. Is it a deal?'

'Yes,' she said, dazed. 'It's a deal.'

'Good, then it's all settled.'

'Not quite. How long do you see this arrangement lasting?'

He frowned, as if puzzled by the question.

'For as long as I say,' he replied at last.

Of course, she thought wryly. What else?

'Now, to details,' he continued briskly. 'As far as anyone else is concerned you're a distant relative of my wife, paying us a visit. Liza calls you Holly, but I see from your passport that your name is Sarah.'

'Yes. Holly's a nickname that my mother gave me when I was five. I put a bit of holly in her bed one Christmas.'

'It's useful. Since the police are looking for Sarah Conroy, you won't attract attention.'

'But if they keep looking—'

'That train was their best chance and they fumbled it,' he said with a shrug. 'Now let us be practical. Take this money. It's your first week's wages. You'll be paid in cash because the less paperwork the better. Is there anything in your purse that has your real name?'

'A credit card.'

'Let me see.'

As soon as she produced it he took it from her and cut it up.

'Hey!' she cried indignantly.

'Anything that connects you with your real name is dangerous.'

'If I'm prepared to take that risk—'

'But you might reflect that the risk isn't only for yourself.'

The words were lightly spoken but they made her pause. He was a judge, concealing a woman fleeing the law. She wasn't the only one in danger.

'You need clothes,' he continued. 'Sit down over there.' He indicated an extra, smaller desk by the wall, on which stood a laptop computer, connected to the internet.

'You're online to a store in Rome,' he said. 'Go through

it and select some items, then I'll arrange for them to be delivered.'

She could see that it was open at women's wear, and connected to an account in his name. All she had to do was add things to the shopping basket. Slowly she began to go through the pages, trying to believe what she was seeing. This was the most expensive store she'd ever come across. Just looking at the prices made her eyes cross.

She grew even more distracted studying the clothes. Underwear, dresses—everything seemed to be made of silk. It was intimidating.

'I'm really looking for something a little more ordinary,' she said. 'More like me.'

'You call yourself ordinary?' he enquired.

'Well, look at me.'

'I am. You make nothing of yourself. You are tall and slim—'

'Skinny, you mean. And flat-chested. Like a board.'

'Give me patience! Is that any way for a woman to talk? There are women modelling on the catwalk shaped exactly like you, and all you can do is run yourself down.'

'I'm not running myself down,' she said huffily. 'I'm being realistic. I'm no beauty.'

'Did I say you were?'

She gaped. 'You said—'

'I said you had a shape you should make the best of, but you don't think that way. You say "thin" when you should say "slim". Your mind-set is askew.'

'Well, pardon me for thinking incorrectly. Obviously an Italian woman would do better, but I can't help being the wrong nationality.'

'You must learn not to put words into my mouth. Don't

blame your nationality. My wife was also English, and she was as conscious of herself and the effect she made as any Italian woman. It's something in here.' He tapped his forehead.

'Oh, I'm conscious of the effect I make,' she said, in a sudden temper. 'Homely is the word. And that's the kind version.'

'No woman with a twenty-two-inch waist is ever homely,' he retorted.

'And my face? It's nothing.'

'All right, it's nothing,' he conceded. 'That's better than being bad.'

'Homely,' she repeated, raising her voice. 'Look, it's my face, I know more about it than you do.'

Why were they having this quarrel? It had sprung up from nowhere and made no sense. But from the deep well of tangled emotions inside her came a tension that had to release itself somehow. So she had turned on him.

Something in his eyes told her it was the same with him. His nerves were as taut as her own, and he too had exploded irrationally.

'I doubt if you know much about it,' he said now, 'or about the person behind it.'

'I know her all right,' she said with bitter emphasis. 'She was so used to being a little brown mouse that she fell for the first pack of lies she was told by a man. There's nothing else to know.'

He didn't reply at once, but considered her for a while before saying slowly, 'I doubt that's true. You've never explored the possibilities, so try to see your face as a blank canvas on which you will write whatever you want to.'

'Is that what your wife did?'

His mouth twisted, though whether with humour or with pain she couldn't have said.

'Now you mention it, yes. She wasn't a great beauty, but

she could make every man believe that she was. When she walked into a room, heads turned.'

'And you didn't mind?'

'No, I—I was proud of her.'

'But I'm not her. I could never be like that.'

'Nobody could ever be like her. Now, let us return to business.'

His tone had become practical again, like that of a man announcing to a meeting that it was time for the next item on the agenda.

'In this house you'll need a decent wardrobe, so forget the kind of thing you're used to and choose clothes that will help you fit in with...' He made a gesture indicating the luxurious surroundings. 'Please hurry up, I have a lot of work to get on with.'

The last of the tension was diffused. She could concentrate on the screen and even enjoy the dizzying array of delightful garments that danced before her.

'Do the job properly,' was his only comment as he seated himself at the other desk.

He had prepared everything efficiently, accessing the English version of the site and calling up a conversion table showing both English and continental sizes.

Her puritanical self made one last effort, pointing out remorselessly that cheap materials had always sufficed in the past. But then she told it to shut up and let her concentrate. After that it was easy.

First, casuals, blouses, sweaters, trousers, all cut with deceptive simplicity, all costing a fortune. After the first shocked glance she didn't concern herself with prices.

Underwear. Satin panties, slips, lacy bras, in white, black, ivory. Here she tried to be a little abstemious, cutting the order down to her barest needs.

She lingered over cocktail dresses, tempted to desperation

over a garment in silky chiffon, cut tight and low both back and front. She could buy it in black or deep, dark crimson.

But she wasn't going to buy it at all, she reminded herself sternly. She was just taking a look.

Coats. Yes. Think sensible! She could justify a light summer coat. This colour. No, that one. But perhaps this one was better.

'Get them both,' said a bored voice passing behind her. She looked up quickly, but he was already re-seating himself at the desk.

She got them both. She was only obeying orders.

'I've finished choosing,' Holly said at last. 'What do I do now?'

'Leave the rest to me. Now, it's late and you've had a long day. I suggest you go to bed.'

'First I should like to see Liza, and say goodnight.'

He checked his watch.

'She should be asleep by now, but she's probably stayed up in the hope of seeing you. Very well. Turn left at the top of the stairs, and it's the second door.'

'Are you coming with me?'

There was a touch of constraint in his manner as he said, 'I've already said goodnight to her.'

'But if she's waited up, I'm sure she'd love to see you again.'

She sensed him about to make an impatient reply. Then he gave a brief nod, as though settling something within himself, and rose to lead the way out of the room.

CHAPTER THREE

As THEY emerged into the hall they heard the sound of argument coming from above. There was Berta's voice, but above that was Liza's, shrill and insistent.

'They're coming, I know they are.'

'But your father has already said goodnight,' Berta protested. 'He's a busy man—'

'He's not too busy for me, he's not, he's not.'

The last words shook Holly to the depths. They were a cry of desperation, as though the child was frantically trying to convince herself of something she needed to believe.

She glanced at the judge, who was standing as if frozen.

'Perhaps this isn't a good idea,' he murmured.

'On the contrary, it's a great idea,' she said quickly. 'Your daughter has just proclaimed her faith in you, and when you go up those stairs she'll know she was right, and that you're not too busy for her.'

She waited for his face to brighten at this simple answer, but he didn't move, and she realised that he was at a total loss. He was a judge, schooled in order, method, decisiveness. And he didn't know what to do with his own unhappy child.

'It's a fantastic chance for you to make her feel better,' she urged. 'If only all life could be that easy. For pity's sake, stop and think.'

In her eagerness she took his arm, realising too late that he would see this as impertinence. But he only glanced at her hand in the second before she snatched it away.

'You're right,' he said.

She thought his voice sounded oddly defeated. But she must surely have imagined that.

'Poppa,' came Liza's delighted shriek from above them.

He looked up, and his mouth stretched in an effortful smile as he began to climb the stairs with Holly.

'Not so noisy, *piccina*,' he said. 'You should be asleep by now.'

'I have to say goodnight to Holly.'

'You'll see plenty of her now that she is staying with us.'

Liza gave a shriek of delight and tried to do a little dance, but her bad leg got in the way, and Holly grasped her to stop her falling. Liza immediately hugged her.

'You're staying for ever and ever,' she crowed.

'No darling, not for ever. Just for a little while.'

'But I want you to stay,' Liza said.

'Holly will be here for some time,' her father put in quietly. 'Don't worry about that.'

Holly flashed him a look, which he met with a quiet, implacable one of his own. There was nothing she could say in front of Liza.

'Now, come on, back to bed,' she told the child in a rallying tone, reaching for her.

'Poppa!' Liza reached for him over Holly's shoulder.

He took her hand and they all moved into the bedroom together. Holly laid her in her bed and gave her a hug. Then her father leaned down and kissed her cheek.

'Be a good girl and go to sleep,' he said briefly, and left the room.

Liza was still holding on to Holly's hand. 'Don't go,' she said.

Berta slipped quietly out of the room, leaving the two of them together. Now Liza snuggled down, contented. Her eyes were closed and her breathing was becoming more even. At last her fingers relaxed enough for Holly to draw her hand away, and tiptoe from the room.

It was dark outside and she almost missed the figure standing there, silent and still. She waited for him to speak, but he only looked at her from the shadows before turning away.

When Holly reached her room she found a buxom young woman turning down her bed.

'I am Nora, your maid,' she said, smiling. 'I have set fresh water by your bed for tonight. Do you prefer tea or coffee in the morning?'

'Tea. Thank you.'

'Then I will wish you *buona notte*. Do you wish me to help you undress?'

'No, thank you.'

She was suddenly desperate to be alone with her thoughts, but she found that they were troublesome companions. What had happened tonight was impossible. It hadn't happened because it could not have done.

Yet in this incredible house all boundaries seemed to fade. If she could only talk to an outsider she might recover her sense of proportion.

She had no close family, but an acquaintance would do, someone back in England who knew her in her real life, maybe even someone who would send help.

There was a telephone by the bed, and, with a sense of relief, she lifted the receiver.

It was dead.

Next morning Nora appeared, bearing a tray with a pot of tea, a jug of milk, a bowl of sugar and a saucer of lemon slices.

'I didn't know how you like your tea,' she explained, 'so I brought everything.'

'Thank you,' Holly murmured, trying to pull the sheet up so that Nora wouldn't see that she had slept naked, having no nightgown.

'Shall I run your bath, or would you prefer a shower?'

'I'll take a shower. It's all right, I can look after myself.'

Nora left the room, having first given something that was perilously like a curtsey.

Holly drank the tea, which had been perfectly made, and went into the bathroom. A shower refreshed her, and when she returned, wrapped in a huge towel, Liza was there, in her wheelchair, with Berta.

'She wished to come here and make you welcome,' Berta said, smiling.

'I could have walked,' Liza insisted.

'Not so early in the day,' Berta said. 'It takes time for you to be strong enough.'

Holly seized her clothes and vanished hastily back into the bathroom. When she emerged the three of them breakfasted together. It was a cheerful meal, but Berta seemed to be working herself up to saying something. At last she found the daring to say,

'Would you mind if I went away for a few hours? I need to do some shopping, and now Liza has you…?' She spread her hands in a pleading gesture.

So this was the reason Berta had accepted her intrusion so easily, Holly thought, amused. She saw the chance of a little extra freedom. She hastened to declare that she and Liza would be fine together, and Berta departed, humming.

'What are we going to do now?' Holly asked when breakfast was over.

'Come and meet Mamma,' Liza said eagerly.

Carol Fallucci's memorial had been erected in a shady corner of the grounds. The first time Holly saw it she had a feeling of something not quite right. She could not have defined it, except to say that she would have expected more restraint from the judge. There was something romantically gothic about this fountain with the marble angel, wings extended, that didn't quite fit with the coolness she had encountered from him.

He must have been deeply in love with his wife to have erected such a monument. She tried to picture him consumed by passionate feeling, but she couldn't do it. Nor could she imagine this self-possessed man in the abandonment of grief.

And yet it must be so. Nothing but the most terrible love and yearning could explain such an extravagant monument. And perhaps it was all the more painful for being so fiercely controlled.

Now Holly understood Liza's reference to 'meeting Mamma'. As with many Italian gravestones, this one carried a picture of the dead person. It showed a woman of about thirty, with fine features that were as exquisitely made-up as her hair was elegantly arranged. She looked exactly the kind of wife that a judge ought to have: sophisticated, assured, beautiful.

A million miles from me, Holly thought wryly. Now, *she* could really have worn those cocktail dresses.

To Liza this place was the nearest thing to happiness. She could come here and sit on the step, or dip her hands in the cool water, and talk about the mother she missed desperately, and who had died just before Christmas.

'"December 21st,"' Holly said, reading the inscription. 'That's the worst possible time. Not that any time would be good, but to happen then—'

She felt a small hand creep into hers and Liza nodded in silent agreement.

'Do you have a Mamma?' she asked after a while.

'Not now. She died almost a year ago.'

'Was that just before Christmas, too?'

'It was last October, but Christmas was my first one without her.'

The silent house, the sudden unwelcome freedom for one whose life had been all duty, the aching emptiness—

'Wasn't there anyone else?'

'No, just the two of us. She'd been ill for a long time.'

Holly didn't want to talk about the long, agonising years watching her mother die by slow degrees. Words rose to her lips, all calculated to divert the conversation down another path and kill it with platitudes.

Then she saw Liza's eyes on her. They were innocent and had a quality of kindness that seemed strange in a child. But this one knew more than any child should, and she deserved honesty.

'The doctors couldn't cure her,' she said. 'So I looked after her.'

'Until she died?'

'Yes, as long as she needed me.'

'But you knew she was going to die,' Liza said with an understanding that was too mature for her years. 'She didn't just vanish—suddenly, when you thought everything was all right.'

'Was that what happened to you?'

Liza nodded.

'We were going on holiday,' she said in a slightly husky voice. 'I remember Mamma packing lots of cases because she said we were going away for longer this time. It was going to be a special Christmas holiday, but we'd never been away at Christmas before.

'It was funny because everything was different. Poppa didn't come to see us off, and he didn't say when he'd join us. I asked Mamma when he'd come but she didn't know.

'And then we were on the train, and Mamma was sort of— jumpy. When I said things, she didn't seem to hear me. A man came and talked to us. I'd never met him before, and I didn't like him much.

'Suddenly there was a loud noise and the train turned over and over. Mamma put her arms about me, and I remember a terrible pain. I clung on to her because I knew she'd keep me safe, and I kept calling Poppa because if he was there he'd look after us both. I cried for him again and again but he didn't come.

'Then I went to sleep and when I woke up I was in hospital, and Mamma was dead. I cried and cried, but I never saw her again.'

'You poor little thing,' Holly murmured.

'If I'd known—I could have said lots of things to her first. I could have told her that I loved her.'

'But she would have known that without words.'

'Maybe. But we had a squabble. I didn't want to go without Poppa and I cried and said I wouldn't go. I was nasty to her on the train. Now I can't ever tell her that I'm sorry.'

'Oh, *piccina*,' Holly said, struck to the heart by the burden the child was carrying. 'None of that matters. People fight but it doesn't mean they don't love each other. She knew that.'

'But I want to tell her.'

'And you can. You can still talk to her in your heart. She knew how much you loved her, and that was more important than any argument. You didn't need to say it, because your love for her was part of her love for you. And when it's like that, it's always there.'

'Really?'

'Really.'

Liza nodded. She seemed satisfied, as though anything her new friend said could always be trusted. Holly knew a slight qualm. This appealing child was laying too many expectations on her, and it might lead to her getting even more hurt.

'What was your *mamma* like?' Liza wanted to know.

'She was brave. In spite of what was happening to her, she always found something to laugh about. That's what I remember most—how she laughed.'

Something caught in her throat as the memories of that laughter came back to her, frail, growing shakier but more defiant, until at last it was gone forever. She turned her head to hide the sudden rush of tears, but Liza was too quick for her. In a moment her arms were about Holly's neck, the comforter, not the comforted.

Holly tried to speak but the ache in her throat was too much. At last she gave up and hugged the little girl back, accepting the consolation she offered.

'Perhaps we should go back to the house now,' Holly said at last. 'Aren't you supposed to have a nap?'

'Berta says so,' Liza grumbled, making a face. 'She wants me to use my wheelchair all the time, but I don't need it.'

'I think you need it sometimes. And if you don't rest enough you'll delay your recovery. And then I'll be in trouble,' she added lightly.

Liza scowled but got back into the wheelchair. As they headed home they saw Anna approaching them.

'There's a parcel for you,' she called.

'Already?' Holly said. 'I thought it would be several days.'

'What is it?' Liza asked eagerly.

'My new clothes. Your father made me order some last night because all mine were left on the train.'

'Let's go and see them.'

Back in the house she almost dragged Holly into the tiny lift that had been installed for her, and then into her room, where Anna had laid out the parcel. The child plunged into the delightful business of unpacking, sighing over the lovely clothes.

'This is the best store in all Rome,' she enthused. 'Mamma shopped there all the time. Poppa complained she was always going over the limit of his account, but he didn't really mind because he said she looked so lovely.'

'Well, these clothes aren't to make me look nice,' Holly said firmly, lifting out sweaters, followed by a coat. 'They're practical.'

But then she discovered something that made her frown. Conscious that she was spending the judge's money, she had placed only a modest order of underwear. But there were three times as many panties, bras and slips as she had specified.

Perhaps she had made a mistake, and asked for more than she'd intended. But inwardly she knew this was Signor Fallucci's doing. Before finalising matters, he had reviewed her order and increased it.

But only the underwear. Nothing else had been changed.

She wanted to laugh wildly. He, a judge, had saved her from the police, and within a few hours he was dictating to her in the matter of underwear. There was a surreal quality to it that made her dizzy.

He'd been right. She hadn't ordered enough and he'd known it, but there was an intimacy about such knowledge that gave her an uncomfortable suspicion that she was blushing.

Then she noticed something on the accompanying paperwork that she'd missed before:

'First part of order. Second part to follow soon.'

First part? But everything she'd ordered was here.

The sooner she spoke to him the better.

He didn't appear at supper that evening, and Anna explained that the judge had called to say he was detained by urgent business.

Berta had returned, glowing from her day out, and the three of them had supper together.

'Did you do all the shopping you wanted?' Holly asked.

'Yes, I bought lots of lovely new clothes.' Berta sighed happily.

'Will Alfio like them?' Liza asked cheekily.

'I don't know what you mean,' Berta said, trying to sound airy.

'Alfio's her sweetheart,' Liza confided to Holly. 'He works in the hospital and—'

'And that's enough out of you,' Berta said, going pink. 'Besides, he's not my sweetheart. He's—' her happiness came bursting out '—he's my fiancé.'

The rest of the meal was taken up with a detailed description of the proposal she had received a few hours earlier, a conversation which they all enjoyed.

That night Holly donned one of her new nightgowns. It was flimsy and delicate, with a feel of such luxury that it seemed almost criminal to wear it in solitude. She thought of the plain cotton pyjamas that had always suited her before, and wondered if she would ever be satisfied with them again.

Sleeping in such luxury was a new, sensual experience. So was waking up in it. There was another sensual experience when she put on the new underwear, feeling it move softly against her skin. It was designed for sexual enticement, to persuade a man to remove it, and Holly could feel it mysteriously transforming her. Only a certain kind of woman could wear this underwear. She was wearing it. Therefore she was that woman. The logic of it was perfect.

'I'm going crazy,' she murmured, trying to clear her head. 'This place is getting to me. Or perhaps it's the heat.'

Already at this early hour, she could sense the promise of the searing-hot day to come. It hadn't been like that before she got into the train. In the little town that she'd fled the weather had been warm but benign. It was only now that the heatwave had descended, so that even the early hours glowed with the anticipation of the furnace to come.

The judge made only a brief appearance at breakfast, but when he left the table she followed him to his study. He was putting papers into his briefcase.

'I'm in a hurry,' he said, without looking up. 'Is it urgent?'

'It is to me,' she said firmly, advancing into the room. 'I received my clothes from the store but...'

It had been so easy when she'd rehearsed the speech, but face to face with this cool, ruthless man, her nerve gave way. How could she ever have imagined she could discuss her underwear with him?

'It contains more than I ordered,' she managed to say.

He shrugged. 'You didn't order enough. I appreciate your attempt at economy but it was needless.'

'But I can't allow you to—'

'*Signorina*, the question of you allowing me to do anything does not arise, since you're in no position to stop me.'

'That's right, rub my nose in it.'

'*Scusi*? Rub your nose?'

'It's an English expression. It means that you're making me feel helpless. I don't like it.'

'Most women don't object when a man buys them clothes,' he said, sounding a little bored.

'That depends on the clothes. I do object to you buying me underwear. We don't have the kind of relationship that...'

Seething, she fell silent. He was regarding her with eyebrows raised satirically.

'There's more than one kind of relationship,' he said. 'If you're afraid that I shall try to "take advantage" I believe is the term, you need not be.'

He said the last few words with a slow, savage emphasis that chilled her. He was reminding her of his recent bereavement, saying that if she thought she could interest him she flattered herself. Embarrassment held her silent.

'If there's nothing more...' he said.

'I also think you should return my passport. Being without it makes me feel like a prisoner.'

'That is nonsense,' he said calmly. 'If you want to leave you have only to contact the British Consul and ask for their help. You'll be provided with an identity card that will get you back to England. Here's the address.'

He scribbled on a sheet of paper and handed it to her.

'If you wish I can call them now and use all my influence to ensure that things are made smooth for you.'

It was all true, Holly realised. She could do exactly what he had described. But all this reasonableness didn't dispel her suspicions. The reference to his influence sounded helpful but was actually a subtle reminder that he was in control here, even when it didn't look like it.

The time had come to stand up for herself.

'Well, maybe I'll go to the consulate today,' she said firmly.

'I'll order the car for you.'

'No, thank you, I'll make my own way there.'

'Then I'll call a taxi.' With a touch of exasperation he added, 'Or would you prefer to walk several miles?'

'If necessary,' she retorted, in a fury.

He groaned. 'Enough of this. Must we have these trials of strength?'

'Maybe your strength alarms me.'

'Have the honesty to admit that I've exercised it in your defence.'

'Because I'm useful to you.'

'Certainly you are, just as I am useful to you. The best bargains are those where both sides gain.'

Everything he said made perfect sense, and she would have liked to thump him for it.

'But I wouldn't dream of detaining you against your will,' he added. 'Go if you want to.'

She was saved from having to answer by the door opening and a small head peering round.

'Can I come in, Poppa?'

'Of course.' He rose and went to the door, giving his arm to help Liza walk.

'I was looking for Holly.'

'Well, here she is.'

Liza pulled herself free from her father to limp forward at a run.

'You vanished,' she said in a tense voice. 'I thought you'd gone away for ever and ever.'

And that was her nightmare, Holly realised, conscience-stricken.

'No, darling,' she said, dropping to her knees so that she could meet Liza's eyes on a level. 'I just came to talk to your father. I'm sorry, I should have told you first, so that you didn't worry. I haven't gone away.'

She pulled Liza towards her in a bear hug, and found herself almost suffocated in the returning embrace.

'And you won't, will you?' Liza begged.

The decision was already made. Liza was the one who had first championed her, and now she owed the little girl a debt. Going to the consulate would have to wait.

She looked up at the judge, expecting to see an expression of cool triumph, or even indifference at a victory he would have taken for granted.

But there was something else there. Instead of assurance, there was apprehension. Instead of authority, she saw pleading.

That must be a mistake. Not pleading. Not this man who had her in his power.

But it was in his eyes and the taut lines of his whole body. Her decision mattered to him desperately, and he was full of terrible tension waiting for it.

'No, I won't go away,' she said. 'I'll stay as long as you want me.'

'For ever and ever?' Liza asked.

'For ever and ever.'

'I think it's time I was leaving for work,' he said in a voice that sounded strained.

'Come on,' Holly said, laying a hand on Liza's shoulder and shepherding her out of the room.

There were still battles to be fought, but this wasn't the time or place.

CHAPTER FOUR

DESPITE her troubles, Holly found it easy to settle into the life of the villa, which seemed to open its arms to welcome her. Everything was done for her comfort. The maid cleaned her room and made her bed, leaving her free to spend her time with Liza.

Nothing mattered but the little girl who had clung to her so desperately on the train, weeping as though her heart would break. As she had guessed, Liza's spirits were volatile. She could be happy one minute and tearful the next. Even worse were the fits of screaming that would overtake her without warning.

'I nursed her in hospital,' Berta explained. 'When she was ready to leave she still needed care at home, and they thought I'd be best because she was used to me. She's a sweet child, but I can't cope with her outbursts. They're alarming because they seem to come out of nowhere.'

'But really they come out of her tragedy,' Holly suggested. 'To lose her mother like that—the train crash, her injury... She must still be suffering a lot.'

'To be sure. I understand it well enough,' Berta agreed. 'I just don't seem to be any help to her. I put my arms round her and try to console her, but it doesn't make any difference. I'm not the one she wants.'

'It's her mother that she wants, poor little soul,' Holly sighed.

'Yes, but, failing that, someone like her. Someone English, like her *mamma*. You.'

This seemed to be the answer. Only that morning Liza had become violently upset about some trivial matter that had arisen over breakfast. But then the mood had passed so quickly that Holly had barely understood what had brought it on. She'd asked no more questions, unwilling to prolong what was best forgotten.

Holly studied the child constantly to discern more about her needs, but almost equally useful were the talks she had with Berta and Anna during the afternoons, when Liza took her nap.

Since the judge often left early and came home late it was almost as though he wasn't there at all, so they talked freely.

'When he is here he shuts himself away,' Anna observed one day in the kitchen as she poured coffee for the three of them. 'He didn't used to be like that, before his wife died. But now it's like living with a ghost.'

'What was she like?' Holly asked.

'Beautiful,' Anna said enviously. 'Like a model. It was easy to see why he was mad about her.'

'Mad about her?' Holly queried. Such a picture didn't sort with the harsh, unyielding man she knew.

'Mad, insane, crazy,' Anna said firmly. 'I know it's hard to believe if you've only seen him now, but in those days he was all smiles, all happiness. I came to work here soon after they married and I tell you, you never saw a man so much in love. He would have died for her. Instead…' she sighed.

'I was on duty in the hospital the day of the accident,' Berta recalled. 'I saw him walk in, and he showed nothing. No emotion, nothing at all. His face was blank.'

'Did he know his wife was already dead?' Holly asked.

'Yes. The first thing he said to the doctor was, "Even if she's dead, I want to see her", and the doctor didn't like that because she looked very bad, all smashed up. He tried to make him wait a while, and I saw his face become even colder and harder as he said, "I want to see her, do you understand?"'

'He can be scary when he's enraged,' Anna mused. 'Did the doctor give way?'

'Not at once. He said that the little girl was still alive and perhaps he'd like to see his daughter first. And Signor Fallucci said, 'I demand to see my wife, and if you don't get out of my way you'll be sorry.'

'So the doctor showed him into the room. The judge ordered everyone out so that he'd be alone with her, but when we were outside the doctor told me to stay close, and fetch him when Signor Fallucci came out, or if "anything happened" as he put it.'

'So you went and listened at the door,' Anna said wryly.

'Well—yes, all right, I did.'

'And what did you hear?'

'Nothing. There wasn't a sound from inside that room. I've seen people visiting the dead. They cry, or call out the person's name, but all I heard was silence. When he came out—his face—I'll never forget it. You'd have thought he was the dead one.'

'Did he go to see Liza then?' Holly asked curiously.

'Yes, I took him in. She looked terrible, attached to all those machines. I was going to tell him not to touch her, but I didn't have to. He never moved, just stood staring at her as though he didn't know who she was. Then he turned and walked out.'

'I don't understand that,' Anna said. 'He's always adored her, almost as much as his wife. I heard someone make a joke with him once, about how he'd feel differently when he had a son. And he said, "Who needs a son? No child could mean more to me than my Liza." I'll never forget the way he said that, or his face as he looked at her.'

'Well, he wasn't like that in the hospital,' Berta said. 'Mind you, men can't cope with that sort of thing as we do. Even the strongest of them get scared and freeze up.'

It might be true, yet somehow Holly wasn't satisfied with this facile explanation. There was a mystery here, the same mystery as the one that made Signor Matteo Fallucci, a judge with a career and a reputation at stake, harbour a suspicious character for the sake of a child he seldom saw.

On the one hand, there was the love so vast that it would take any risk. On the other hand, there was the frozen withdrawal. If she could understand that, then perhaps she would begin to understand him.

But she did not think he was a man who could be easily understood. She was even more sure of it a moment later when Anna said,

'He never speaks of her. The only one who's allowed to mention her name is Liza, and even then he steers her off the subject as soon as he can.'

'But that's terrible,' Holly said, disturbed. 'He's the person who knew his wife best, and Liza needs to discuss her mother with him.'

'I know,' Anna said sympathetically. 'But he can't make himself do it. And he doesn't even have the *signora's* picture on his desk. He doesn't act like a grieving widower at all, and yet he must be, because he built that fancy monument, and he keeps going to it, as though he couldn't keep away.'

'Night after night,' Berta confirmed.

'One night I was out there,' Anna remembered, 'and I saw him close enough to tell that he was talking to her. It was really scary.'

'You'd better not let him know you spy on him,' Berta said darkly. 'That would be the end of you.'

'I know. I dashed off before he spotted me.'

Berta was so delighted with Holly's coming that she asked no awkward questions, almost as though she had a superstitious fear that to query her good luck would make it vanish.

She gladly showed Holly the mechanical part of caring for Liza. A physiotherapist attended twice a week, and from her Holly learned some simple exercises to be repeated every day. She mastered them without trouble, and Liza was more relaxed with her.

To show her preference she insisted on talking English with Holly, even when Berta was there.

'That's not very polite to Berta,' Holly protested. 'Her English isn't too good.'

'Non e importante,' Berta said with a grin. 'Tonight I see my Alfio, and we don't talk English.'

Holly went regularly to the library to study the newspapers that were put there every day, to see if there was any mention of herself. But there was nothing.

Like every other room in the house this one was luxurious, furnished with ornate oak bookshelves that came from another age. The volumes were mostly history, philosophy and science. Some of them were very old, suggesting a family that had collected books for centuries.

She had the answer in a portrait of two ladies, dressed in the style of a hundred years ago, both of whose faces so strongly resembled the judge's that it was clear he was their descendant. A small plaque at the bottom announced that this was the Contessa d'Arelio, and her daughter, Isabella.

'That's his grandmother,' Anna said, coming in with a

duster. 'The younger lady, I mean. She married Alfonso Fallucci. They say there was a terrible row because her family wanted her to marry a title.'

'Alfonso wasn't good enough for them?' Holly asked.

'They thought he was a nobody, but she insisted on marrying him. She was right, too, because he made a fortune in shipping.'

So that explained how he came to be living in this extravagant place, far beyond what most judges could afford. Much of it was shut off, the rooms surplus to such a small family, but what she could see was still sumptuous, both inside and out.

A small army of gardeners worked in the grounds. There was one whose first duty was to care for the memorial to Carol Fallucci, keeping the fountain clean and flowing freely, and the flower beds perfect. Taking a stroll that afternoon, Holly saw him busily weeding, and exchanged a smile and a wave.

Walking on further, she came to a sight that checked her. Here was a small swimming pool, surrounded by trees and invisible from the house. It would have been perfect for a summer afternoon, except that it was empty and neglected.

Empty and neglected. The words repeated themselves inside her head. In some mysterious way they seemed to apply to this place, despite the extensive staff keeping it in order. It was an emptiness of the soul, and nobody was more afflicted by it than the master of the house.

She wondered how she was so sure of this, since she barely knew him, but she had no doubt.

Liza's most treasured possession was a book of photographs, containing everything, starting with the wedding of Matteo and Carol Fallucci. There were pictures of them with their newborn baby, their year-old baby, and so on.

It was his face that caught her attention. Carol would some-times look at him, sometimes at her child, but most often she looked directly at the camera. The judge did this only once. His eyes were for the two women in his life, always with a look of blatant worship. In one he rested his cheek against Carol's hair, as though here lay all joy and contentment.

Some of the pictures showed the family gathered around a swimming pool, all in bathing costumes. Carol was at her most glamorous, in a black bikini designed to show off her glorious figure, her fair hair tumbling over her shoulders. Sitting beside her was Liza, sturdy and cheerfully belligerent, her face so much like her mother's that the effect was startling.

And there he was, Matteo, as Holly could never have imagined him, lean and lithe in swimming trunks. A stranger, seeing the breadth of his shoulders, his flat stomach and muscular arms and legs, would have put him down as an actor or a model. But not a judge, she thought wryly. Anything but a judge.

Neither did his face belong in a courtroom. This was a healthy, handsome man, with powerful enjoyment of life and a desire to savour every moment.

The picture that really transfixed her showed Liza and her father, gazing into each other's eyes, both of them blissfully, adoringly happy, oblivious to the rest of the world.

That was what it must be like to have a father, she thought.

From Liza's appearance the picture must have been taken the previous summer, yet Matteo looked years younger. His smile was that of a completely different man; one still young, blazing with hope and happiness. He had almost nothing in common with the man he was now.

Holly felt she began to understand him. His beloved wife had died, leaving him sunk in despair. He would find it hard to confide in anyone, and the exaggerated monument in the garden was his only way of showing his feelings.

Even Liza was somehow lost to him, as though his heart had frozen too much to let him respond to her needs. They might have consoled each other, but he was reduced to commandeering help from a stranger. He wasn't an easy man to like, but she found that her heart mysteriously ached for him.

Then she looked again and realised why the pool seemed familiar. It was the one she'd seen in the grounds. So glitteringly joyous then, so desolate now. It seemed to sum up the change that had come over this house when the woman who was its heart had died, leaving her husband and child bereft, yet unable to communicate.

As she returned to the house Berta waylaid her.

'The judge is home,' she said. 'He's with Liza and he said not to disturb him.' She looked around before asking in a conspiratorial voice, 'That online catalogue you were looking at—did it have any wedding dresses at reasonable prices?'

'It didn't have anything at reasonable prices,' Holly said. 'I've never been so scared in my life. So, you've reached the stage of choosing a wedding dress?'

Berta needed no encouragement to talk about her fiancé. Holly smiled but this was a hard conversation for her. Only recently she too had been planning a wedding to a man who made her pulses race, a man she thought she would adore all her life—until he betrayed her in the most brutal, selfish manner.

He had never loved her, she knew that now. Instead he had laid a cynical trap for her, and she had fallen into it without the slightest caution.

Where was he now? What was he doing? Would she ever see him again?

* * *

Matteo was there at supper. Several times she caught him watching her curiously, and she began to feel that something had gone badly wrong. Her fears seemed to be confirmed when he rose from the table and spoke to her quietly.

'When Liza is asleep, please come to my study, no matter how late it is.'

It was a couple of hours before she was ready to leave the child, but when Liza was breathing regularly she crept out of the room and downstairs to the study.

When there was no answer to her knock she pushed open the door gently. She couldn't see him, but she decided to go in anyway.

The lights were low and she had to look around to be sure he wasn't there. When there was no sign of him she looked around as much as she could, and that was how she noticed the newspaper on the desk.

It was lying open under the only bright light, the desk lamp. At first she saw it upside down and the only word that registered was *Vanelli*.

A name she knew, to her everlasting bitterness.

Moving as in a dream, she lifted the newspaper and fought to read through the words that danced before her eyes. Only the gist of it reached her.

Valuable miniature—worth millions—replaced by a cheap copy—duo of thieves, Sarah Conroy and Bruno Vanelli— Vanelli arrested but escaped—no trace of the woman...

She sat down suddenly, feeling the breath knocked out of her body.

It had been bound to happen. She'd been living in a fool's paradise, but it couldn't last. The brutal truth had caught up with her. At best she would be thrown out. At worst she would be arrested. She must run. But where? There was nowhere to run to.

There was a photograph of Bruno in the paper. Not knowing why, she ran her fingers over the handsome, wilful face. It was just as she had first seen it, the charming quirk at the corner of the mouth, the roguish glint in the eye. How she had loved it when that glint had been turned on her. How her heart had thundered!

She touched the picture again, feeling the dead paper beneath her fingers, trying to conjure him up as he had first appeared to her. But that dream was dead. Tears stung her eyes and began to slide down her cheeks.

'Is it a good likeness?'

The judge was standing there, watching her, as he must have been for the last few minutes. Hastily she brushed the tears away.

'Yes, it's a good likeness,' she whispered. 'You didn't leave this here by accident, did you?'

'Of course not. I had to know.'

'Now that you know, what are you going to do?'

'I'm not sure. There's a lot I need to understand first.'

'You mean, like—am I a crook? If I deny it, will you believe me?'

'I might.'

'And if you don't—what then? What of Liza?' she asked.

In the poor light she saw him flinch.

'I've been talking to her,' he said. 'She has much to say about you, especially about your mother.'

'My mother? What does she have to do with this?'

'She could have a lot to do with it. I understand that she was ill, and you had to look after her.'

'Yes. She had a wasting disease. I knew she'd never get

better. For the last ten years of her life she needed constant attention, so I stayed at home to care for her.'

'There was nobody else? Your father?'

'I never knew him. My parents weren't married, and when she became pregnant he just vanished. I never knew anyone from his side of the family. I didn't know much of my mother's family either. I think they were ashamed of her, and they never helped.

'So for years it was just the two of us, and we were happy. When I showed a talent for drawing she arranged for me to have special lessons, although they were expensive. She took on two and sometimes three jobs to make the extra money. She dreamed of sending me to art college even more than I dreamed of it, but before I could go she was already showing signs of illness. So I did a teacher training course instead.

'When I finished that, I got a job in a local school, but I was only there two terms before I had to leave to be with her.'

'That must have been hard on you, having your life swallowed up.'

'I never saw it like that. I loved her. I wanted to be there for her as she'd been there for me. But why am I telling you all this? What does this have to do with—?'

'Just answer my questions,' he said curtly. 'I'm beginning to get the picture. It must have been a very restricted existence. Did you go out, have boyfriends?'

'Not really. Boyfriends didn't want to know about Mom.'

'How did you come to be visiting Portsmouth?'

'I had a friend who lived there. I met her when I was on my course. She used to invite me every year and Mom was determined I should have a holiday, so she insisted on going into respite care to let me have a break.'

'And how long did that last?'

'Until last year, when she died.'

Her voice shook on the last words and she fell silent. He was silent too, not offering sympathy, which could hardly be genuine, and which she would have found it hard to cope with, but letting her take her time.

'And then?' he asked at last in a voice that was quiet, and almost gentle.

'I took a refresher course so that I could start teaching and that's when I met—'

'Bruno Vanelli.'

'Yes.'

'And you fell for him because you'd never learned to be worldly-wise. I didn't understand that until I spoke to Liza, and discovered that your life had given you little experience of the world, and of men. But why didn't you tell me yourself?'

'Didn't we agree that the less I told you the better?'

'True.'

She gave a brief, mirthless laugh. 'Anyway, there isn't much to tell. He sought me out. He was good-looking and I was flattered. And it seemed so romantic that he was Italian. That's how stupid I was.'

'Ah, yes, we have that image,' he murmured ironically.

'If I'd been a bit sharper I'd have known that the truth is different—nothing to do with *amore*.'

'And what do you think the truth is?'

'It's a stiletto,' she said bitterly, 'a slim dagger, small enough to be concealed until the last moment. And then it slides in so smoothly, so easily, so cruelly. And the victim never sees it coming until it's too late.'

Matteo gave a crack of laughter that, had she been in the mood to notice, matched her own in bitterness.

'That may sometimes be true, *signorina*, but not always. It can be the poor, crazy Italian who is deluded, and the English enemy who deceives and tortures. The blow is so unexpected that it seems to come out of the sunshine, but afterwards there is only darkness. Where we use a stiletto, you use a bludgeon, but the destruction is just as final.'

Holly stared at him as it dawned on her that this was no idle speculation. He was speaking out of a savage misery as deep as her own.

'Do *you* have an English enemy?' she asked.

She saw him stop, tense and control himself before saying, 'Go on telling me about Bruno Vanelli.'

'I'm sorry, I didn't mean—'

'*I said go on.*' His voice was harsh.

Something had happened. She wasn't sure what, but the air was jagged with anguish.

'Go on,' he said again, more calmly. 'I need to hear the rest.'

She turned away, trying to escape the force of his presence. Now the hardest part of the story confronted her, and she could feel her courage ebbing away. It had been painful enough to live it. To relive it was more than she could bear.

'Tell me everything,' he commanded.

'No,' she choked, 'not everything.'

'Every last detail that you remember,' he said remorselessly.

When she did not speak he came up behind her and seized her arms, trying to turn her towards him, but she resisted.

'I can't help you through the pain,' he said. 'I can only tell you to endure and not yield to it. It's the only way to survive.'

Something in his voice made her relax, even against her will. He pulled her around to face him and she stood there, too distraught to move. He was watching her carefully, his dark eyes seeming to hold her even more firmly than his hands.

'Yes,' she murmured. 'The only way.'

'So now tell me,' he repeated. 'Everything.'

CHAPTER FIVE

AT LAST Holly nodded and he led her to a chair, urging her down gently, then retreating to stand by the wall a short distance away. After a moment she began to speak.

It was hard to talk about her happiness, now that it was gone for good. She tried to function as a machine, but she was remembering the sweetest time of her life.

'He took me out to dinner, we were together all the time. He seemed to want nothing except to be with me.'

She fell silent as memories assailed her.

When I'm with you, love of my life, I seem to come alive. You're there in my dreams. I think of nobody else.

'He said such things,' she whispered. 'They sounded wonderful—'

'And yet words mean so little,' came his voice from just behind her. 'We all know that in our hearts but we won't let ourselves believe it, because when we do—there is nothing.'

'Well, maybe "nothing" isn't so terrible,' she said, almost angrily. 'Maybe it's best.'

'That depends on what you had before, or what you think you had before.'

'Yes, I suppose it does,' she said heavily. 'I know now that he chose me because I'm good at copying other people's work. He showed me a photograph of a miniature that he said belonged to his family and asked me to imitate it. He said the original was kept in a bank, because it was so valuable.

'Then he invited me to come to Italy with him, to meet his family in a little town near Rome, called Roccasecca. I'd never heard of it before but when I got there I loved it. It was just like every romantic picture I'd ever seen of a small Italian town. I should have realised it was too perfect to be true.

'When we got there, the family seemed to disappear. There was always some reason why the meeting had to be postponed, although he took the picture to them and told me they loved it.

'I suppose I began to be suspicious then, but I tried to ignore it. It had been a lovely dream and I couldn't face the fact that it was over—no, it wasn't over. It had never started. It had been false from the beginning. He'd played me for a sucker, and boy, was I ever a sucker!'

She gave a hard laugh, looking into the distance, remembering.

'I was the love of his life, his angel,' her lips twisted in irony aimed at herself, 'his beloved. Imagine that! Oh, I believed it. I ached to believe it. All the tired old clichés, *amore, mia bella per l'eternità* . And all the time his brain was calculating like a cash register.'

Holly stopped again, but held out a hand to ward him off, lest he dared insult her with sympathy. But he didn't, only watched her with wary eyes.

'I must have seen it then,' she said at last, 'but I blinded myself to the truth a little longer. After all, there was nothing specific, just vague suspicions. Then he told me to go home, and he'd join me later.

'My flight left from Rome, so I had to get the train from Roccasecca. Bruno dropped me off at the railway station but he didn't stay, even though there was a two-hour wait for the train. I guess he was anxious to get away from me. While I waited I remembered something I thought I'd left behind in my room. I checked my luggage, and that was when I found it.'

'The original of the miniature?'

'How did you know?'

'It was fairly obvious where this story was leading. As you say, he came looking for a talented artist with a gift for copying. He chose England because he isn't known there, plus you would be useful in getting the real picture out of Italy.'

'It sounds so obvious,' she said with a sigh.

'Obvious to me, perhaps, but there's no need for you to be so hard on yourself. What did you do next?'

'I didn't know what to do, so of course I did the wrong thing. I called him and told him what I'd found. He tried to sweet-talk me, and the more he talked, the more scared I became. I hung up. Then I ran out of the station, got rid of the picture, and went back.'

'That wasn't wise. You should have gone in the other direction.'

'I know, but I'd left my luggage at the station. And when I got there the train was due out in ten minutes. It seemed best to get on it. I didn't think anyone's suspicions could have been aroused by then,' she explained.

'Bruno Vanelli is known in that area. He has a criminal record, and when that miniature vanished he was the first one they thought of. He was never more than one step ahead but he could have been safe if you'd got the picture out of the country. Hence his rush.'

'But if you know all this, why am I telling you?'

'Because there's a missing piece of the puzzle that only you know. Exactly where did you leave the picture?'

Holly rose hastily and began to pace the floor, torn two ways, but he stopped her, fixing her with a gaze from his dark, brilliant eyes.

It came over her, with frightening intensity, how much trust she was being asked to put in this man. He was an officer of the law. If she told him what he wanted to know, what would happen next? Were the police waiting for her with handcuffs?

She looked up, terrified, and after a moment he nodded.

'You have to trust me,' he said. 'I know that your experience has left you mistrustful, but if you don't trust me, what will you do?'

'I don't know,' she whispered.

Something in her rebelled at this situation. Inch by inch she was being drawn under his control and she would fight that to her last breath.

'*I don't know*,' she cried.

Matteo took hold of her. His hands were hard and warm, reassuring even as they commanded.

'Trust me,' he said softly. 'You must trust me. You do, don't you?'

'I—'

'Tell me that you trust me. *Say it*.'

'Yes,' she whispered. She hardly knew she was saying the words. Something stronger than herself had taken her over, and it was no use fighting. She felt hypnotised.

'Tell me where you left that package.'

'There was a little church near the station,' she said, trying to speak through her confused thoughts. 'It's very tiny with a—'

'I know it well. I have friends in Roccasecca. Liza and I were visiting them, which is how we came to be on the same train. Go on.'

'The church was empty when I went in, so I put the picture behind the altar. There's a curtain covering a wall with a hole at the bottom. I slipped it in there.'

'Are you telling me the truth?'

'Yes—yes—'

'Have you left anything out? Think hard.'

'No, I put it there, I swear I did.'

At last he released her. 'If you're lying—heaven help us both.'

'I'm not lying. But someone might have found it by now.'

'Let's hope not. You've been luckier than you know. Roccasecca was the birthplace of a mediaeval saint. The picture is reputed to be him, and it belongs to the very church where you left it. If we can find it, we can argue that no theft was committed, since it was returned to its rightful owners.'

'But what can you do?'

'I won't let anything happen to you. I need you too much. You are useful to me as nobody else can be. *Because of that* you can trust me to defend and protect you as nobody else would do.' He gave a wry smile. 'Selfish motives are always dependable. Remember that, and feel safe.'

She nodded. It was true.

'So, if the picture's still there, I'm going to arrange for it to be discovered, without involving you.'

'But how?'

He shrugged. 'An anonymous message, maybe. Now, I suggest that you go to bed and forget about everything that's been said tonight.'

'But suppose—'

'Suppose nothing,' he said firmly. 'Forget tonight. Don't

allow yourself to brood. That is where madness lies. None of us know what the future holds.'

Next morning Matteo left the house saying he would be away for a couple of nights. He did not speak to Holly before he left, not even a goodbye, and she had no logical reason for believing that his departure was anything to do with her.

She knew at once that Liza was upset by his absence, and gave herself even more completely than usual to the task of keeping her thoughts occupied. Liza asked again and again where her father had gone. Holly and Berta both reassured her that his journey was necessary 'for work', and she would calm down for a while, only to ask a few moments later, 'He is coming back, isn't he? You promise?'

When she finally fell asleep that night Holly went to her own bed, exhausted and worried. She only slept a short while before being shaken awake by Berta.

'You must come at once. She awoke with a nightmare and I can't comfort her.'

In Liza's room Holly wasted no time with words, but simply got into bed with the child and hugged her until she fell asleep. As she lay holding her in the darkness she was coming to a decision.

Next morning she said to Berta, 'Your room's right next to Liza's, isn't it?'

'So that I am always close if she needs me.'

'Will you change rooms with me?'

'But, *signora,* you are in the best guest room at the judge's orders. He will be angry with me.'

'Leave him to me,' Holly said simply.

By the time Matteo arrived home next evening the

transfer was complete. As she had promised, Holly took care of the matter.

'Liza's happier now I'm on hand all the time,' she said. 'In fact I've had the bed moved into her room, so I'll just use mine as a dressing room. I hope that's all right with you.'

He nodded. 'I bow to your wisdom. Do what you think right. But I wanted you to have somewhere better.'

'It's the best of all, from Liza's point of view. Does anything else matter but that?'

'Of course not. I leave such decisions to you.'

'Berta will be glad to hear that,' she told him cheerfully. 'She was nervous about taking my old room, but I assured her that you wouldn't object.'

'Oh, you did, did you?' he said ironically.

'She won't be there long. Alfio is pressing her to name the day.'

'Then all problems will be solved,' he said lightly.

'Not quite all. Did you—have a successful trip?'

'Entirely successful, thank you. You might say that I went on a hunting expedition.'

'And your quarry?'

'That was found where I'd hoped and is now safely back with its rightful owner.'

The relief was overwhelming, but she forced herself to be realistic.

'What will happen now—to—?'

'Your friend? For the moment nothing. He was granted bail in the hope that he would lead the police to the stolen goods, but he vanished. With luck he might never be heard of again.'

She nodded. 'If he hears that it's been recovered—'

'He won't. I pulled some strings with friends in the locality, and managed to get it kept quiet.'

'But what about Sarah Conway?' she asked cautiously.

'Sarah who? She doesn't exist, according to the police. Vanelli invented her to get the heat off himself. They're not wasting valuable resources looking for a chimera.'

She closed her eyes, faint with relief.

'Thank you,' she murmured. 'Thank you, thank you.'

Holly took a long, deep breath, suddenly aware of a weakness that threatened to consume her. He was telling her that the worst was over, and so it was. The realisation that the fear and dread had ended so abruptly was almost frightening.

And it had happened because he had willed it so. That was almost the scariest thing of all.

'Holly?' His voice sounded close, and when she opened her eyes he was standing right beside her, his eyes alarmed.

The force of conflicting feelings fighting for supremacy shook her to the core, making her sway. Instantly his hands were on her shoulders.

'Are you all right?'

'Yes,' she said, a little breathlessly. 'I'm fine—really—'

'You're not going to faint, are you?' he asked, scandalised.

'Of course not,' she declared indignantly. 'What do you think I am?'

'Someone who's entitled to faint if she wants to,' he answered in a surprisingly gentle voice. 'Someone who has been through enough to undermine the strongest woman, who was determined not to let her courage fail, and who had given everything in her to making sure that it didn't.'

'So what's wrong with that?'

'Nothing, but there's a price to be paid in weakness and misery. Nobody can be strong forever. How many nights have you lain awake devoting your thoughts to Liza instead of your own troubles?'

'Many,' she murmured.

'You were trying to forget the troubles, but now they have to be faced.'

'But I thought they were over.'

'Mostly they are. But they'll haunt you and you can't run from them. Don't try. There's no escape. They have to be struggled through in your head just as you struggled through them in reality.'

As sometimes before, she had the sensation that he was talking about himself as much as her.

'How long will they live with me?' she wondered.

'All your life because now they *are* you. They've changed you into another person and you can't go back.'

'That's true. And I don't want to go back.'

He nodded. 'You're wise. The joy you once had—'

'Thought I had—'

'Is gone forever.'

'But there'll be other happiness,' she said, almost pleading.

'Perhaps, but never as you knew before. Live without it. Be strong without it, but never waste time grieving for it.'

Holly shivered. The strength he was offering was the strength that came from a desert land, because now it was all he knew.

'I wonder if you understand me,' he said softly.

'Yes, I understand you. Goodnight, Signor Fallucci. Thank you for everything you've done.'

As summer advanced and the heat grew more like a furnace, Holly spent more time in the garden, especially in the evenings. One night, about a week after Matteo's return, she slipped out and stood taking long breaths of the night air. There was only a soft moon tonight but she knew her way along the paths to the fountains, guided by their soft splashing, until she came to the memorial.

This was the monument to the love she'd witnessed in the photographs; love as it should be, still powerful after several years of marriage; love that was honest and faithful, that could be trusted until the last moment.

Love such as she had never known, and probably never would.

'Bruno,' she murmured, and on the word a thousand memories crowded in, all beautiful once, all tainted now with bitterness and betrayal.

How his eyes had shone and his smile had seemed for her alone. How skilfully he had inspired sensations she had thought never to feel. How easily she had taken the illusion for the reality!

Fool! Fool!

She leaned over slightly, looking into the water, seeing her own outline, her face in shadow, and the moon, high in the sky. But then she became aware of something else behind her, something that seemed to shimmer in the water. It might have been an illusion, but the hands on her shoulders were real enough.

She whirled, barely able to gasp his name.

'Bruno!'

'Hush!' His hand was quickly across her mouth to silence her. 'Hush, my love!'

She grew still, staring at him in disbelief. This couldn't be happening. There was the handsome face that had so often made her heart beat faster. It was beating now, not with excitement but with anger.

'You look surprised to see me, *amore*,' he said persuasively. 'Didn't you know I'd come after you?'

'I suppose I did if I'd thought of it. Maybe I just didn't think about you very much.'

'No, you forgot me in a moment,' he said reproachfully. 'How could you do that?'

'I wanted to wipe you out of existence.'

'But you can't, can you?' he said, drawing her into his arms. 'You know that you and I are bound together.'

For a moment she tensed to throw him off. It was curiosity that stopped her. How would his kiss feel now that she knew the truth?

Immediately she knew that everything had changed. The touch that had once thrilled her with its promise now meant nothing. The hands whose caresses had been so exciting moved over her without charm or interest. Everything was dead. As dead as her heart.

But being dead was useful. If you couldn't feel, you couldn't be hurt, and what she needed to do was suddenly easy.

She allowed him to feel her relaxing in his arms and knew that she'd fooled him. He was so conceited that he thought this was going to be easy.

'Holly,' he murmured, 'my Holly…'

Not his. Never again.

'Bruno…' she whispered.

'I knew I'd find you waiting for me. Nothing can come between us—are you still mine?'

'What do you think?' she asked softly.

'I think that now we're together we must never be apart again.'

She pulled away from him. Now the decision was finally taken.

'How did you find me?' she asked.

'I was on the train, with the police.'

'And you told them about me.'

'I had to. I had no choice. They beat me up.'

She faced him, almost laughing. 'I don't think so. Don't

insult my intelligence, Bruno. You did that in the past, but not now. You planted that picture on me, and then betrayed me.'

He sighed and abandoned his first strategy.

'Only because you were stupid about everything,' he said, exasperated. 'None of this was my fault.'

Nothing would ever be his fault, she realised. All that mattered to him was himself, his own needs and feelings. Other people existed only to be useful. She felt a chill run through her as her heart slowed to a pace where she could think. Her thoughts were calm, purposeful, almost scary in their cool resolution.

'How did you know to come to this house?' she asked.

'When the train drew in to Rome I saw you, just for a moment, and I recognised the man you were with. Fallucci tried a friend of mine last year, and I was in court when he passed sentence. Five years. He's a hard man, without mercy. What a joke, you living in his house! Did it take you long to seduce him?'

She reacted too fast for thought, striking him across the face so hard that he nearly fell. He stepped back quickly, his hand to his face, staring at her, shocked.

Holly was aghast at herself. Never before in her life had she lost control. But his easy, cheap judgement had caused a furnace of rage and resentment to explode within her, making her lash out on blind instinct.

She backed off, breathing hard, afraid of this new self and what it was prepared to do.

'I don't think I deserved that,' he said warily. 'When I saw you walking out of that station I could have given you away to the police right then. But I didn't.'

'Of course you didn't. You thought if you could escape from the police you could catch up with me later—'

'So that I could throw myself at your feet—'

'So that you could find out where the picture was—'

'Why must you think the worst of me?'

'Guess.'

He changed tack, putting his arms about her.

'Let's not quarrel. I'm sorry I made you angry. I should-n't have made that remark about seducing him. It's just that you're so beautiful you could seduce any man. I'll bet he's crazy about you already—'

'I'm warning you—'

'All right, I won't say any more. I know you're faithful to me.'

It was almost funny, the way this creature deluded himself. She wanted to laugh wildly.

'You've been brilliant,' he went on, oblivious, 'and now we have everything waiting for us. Just get the picture, and we'll be out of here.'

'What?' She couldn't believe what she was hearing.

'It'll bring us a fortune, but we have to get back to England.' His arms tightened. 'I know you're mad at me, but you'll forgive me.'

Had there ever been a man so conceited? After what he'd done to her, he still believed that he had only to sweet-talk her and she would fall for him again.

From behind her there came a faint noise, but Bruno heard nothing. Absorbed in his performance, he was oblivious to all else. Suddenly she knew what she was going to do. The hot rage that had swept her had died, replaced by a freezing feeling that was delicious.

Time to stop being a little brown mouse. Time to stop taking it and start dishing it out.

'Of course I want to be with you,' she said, giving him a slow smile.

'Then get that picture, quickly.'

'I can't. It isn't here. I hid it.'

'Where?'

'In Roccasecca. I had to dump it somewhere and there was a church next to the station. I hid it behind the altar, in a little hole. It'll still be waiting when someone goes to find it.'

He tensed. 'Describe it to me exactly.'

She did so, watching his face in the moonlight, fascinated to see the perspiration as his excitement increased.

'I've got to get there fast,' he said, trying to pull away.

She made a play of holding on to him.

'Not yet. Stay with me a little. I've missed you so much.'

'And I've missed you,' he said hurriedly, 'but there's no time to lose.'

'But you'll come back for me?' She managed to put a note of pleading in her voice.

'Of course I will.'

'Promise?' she asked urgently.

'I promise, I promise. Now let me go.'

Bruno wrenched himself from her arms and made off down one of the paths. Holly waited until he was out of sight before glancing over her shoulder at the man who was no more than a shadow concealed by the trees, and saying, 'Did you hear all that?'

CHAPTER SIX

'I HEARD enough,' said Matteo, coming out of the shadows.

'I was afraid you'd appear too soon, and spoil it.'

'I wouldn't have spoilt it for the world. How long did you know I was there?'

'Only near the end, but it would have been the same whether you were there or not.'

'I thought it was for my benefit.'

'Some of it.' She added with relish, 'But most of it was for mine.'

In the darkness she couldn't see the curious look he gave her, but she didn't need to. She sensed it with every inch of her body and it filled her with satisfaction.

'What are you going to do now?' she asked, apparently casually.

'I ought to alert the household to pick him up at the gate—or perhaps even the police—'

'No,' she said quickly. 'Let him go.'

'Mio dio!' he said angrily. 'Do you still have a soft heart for him, after the way he betrayed you? Are you mad?'

'A soft heart?' she demanded, outraged. 'You saw what I did.'

'Yes, I've never seen a woman strike a man so hard, with such passion—'

'With such anger.'

'Are they very different? Or are they two sides of the same coin? He had only to hint that you might look at another man, and you were ready to kill him.'

But the 'other man' was Matteo himself. Now she remembered more details of that conversation and she felt herself growing warm all over, as though her whole body was blushing. If he should think she was exerting herself to attract him she would die of shame.

To cool down she went to the monument and plunged her hands into the water, laving it over her face, discovering that once more her heart was pounding with a mysterious excitement that had nothing to do with Bruno.

'I was ready to kill Bruno anyway,' she said, forcing herself to speak sharply. 'I'm not pining for him.'

'I think you are, or you'd see yourself as you might have been, locked up, behind bars. And then you'd want to see him in the same place. Don't yearn for an illusion, Holly. It's a weakness you can't afford. Get free of him *now*.'

'And you think I'll do it like that? I mean to get free, but it's vital that you let me do it my own way.'

'By letting him escape?'

'The way I see it, he'll never escape. You said he didn't know the miniature had been found.'

'Yes, I heard you tell him where it was…' he said slowly as understanding dawned. 'He'll go there…be caught red-handed in the church, seeking something that he'll never find because the police already have it.'

'If you think you should alert the police, you'll do so,' she observed. 'Personally I should prefer to think of him just searching—searching—'

'Fruitlessly,' he murmured. 'He could be there forever.'

'That's what I thought.'

He stood before her and regarded her in the silver light. She met his gaze defiantly.

'*Maria vergine!*' he said with whispered admiration, 'but you're a cool one. So you too carry a stiletto.'

'Not a bludgeon?'

His mouth twisted in irony. 'I expect it'll feel like one to him, but you wielded your knife with alarming skill. I'm sure you're familiar with the term *vendetta*.'

Holly nodded. 'Vengeance. Yes, I know what vendetta is. At least, I thought I knew until tonight.'

'But now you've discovered it for yourself,' he agreed. 'And the reality is sweet, isn't it?'

'Oh, yes,' she murmured, nodding. 'It's very sweet.'

'Not just trading blow for blow,' Matteo said, 'but bringing down disaster on your enemy's head, so that he knows he has more to fear from you than you from him. That is true *vendetta*, and I never saw a more cruelly effective example of it than tonight. My congratulations, Holly. I think you must have some Italian blood in you.'

'Or maybe you've just misjudged the English,' she mused.

'That too is possible. Tell me, did you have no compunction about the fate you were preparing for him?'

'None,' she said harshly. 'None at all. True, there was one moment when I wavered slightly—'

'When he kissed you?'

She shook her head. 'You over-estimate the power of a man's embrace, *signore*.'

He gave a sudden grin. In that strange, cold light it had a wolfish look.

'As do all men, so I've been told. We all believe that we have only to smile, to utter words of love, and the woman falls under our spell. The truth, of course, is that she despises us.'

'It was his kiss that showed me the truth,' she explained. 'The magic was gone, and I could see the real man quite clearly.'

'And then—?'

'And then—' she said slowly, *'ven-de-tta.'*

'I will hope and pray never to incur your wrath,' he said with grim satisfaction.

'No need to hope. I'm in your debt.'

Together they walked back to the house, moving at a leisurely pace, like conspirators who'd brought off a successful coup and knew they could be at ease together.

In his study he poured her a glass of wine, and held it up in salute.

'Magnifico,' he said.

Holly laughed and clinked glasses with him, shaking her head as if in disbelief.

'What is it?' he asked, and she had the satisfaction of knowing that she'd baffled him, and it made him uneasy. 'Why are you looking at me like that?'

'I'm trying to understand what I've just learned about you.'

That bothered him, she was glad to see.

'What—have you learned about me?'

'I've just done something callous, unfeeling; something that nobody with a woman's heart could do. Only a short time ago I loved that man, but tonight I revenged myself and tossed him into outer darkness. *And I enjoyed every moment of it.'*

'I'm beginning to realise that.'

'And you think better of me. Don't try to deny it.'

'I don't want to deny it. Tonight you did several years'

growing up in one hour. I congratulate you. And you weren't heartless. You defended yourself with sharp weapons, and he deserved his punishment.

'Not that it's a very terrible punishment. After a while he'll give up searching and go away. He won't have gained but he won't have lost much either, and he'll get off lightly. Your idea of outer darkness is really quite tame. But you're a beginner. In time you'll learn how to do it properly. But don't ruin it now by blaming yourself. Would it be better to shrink into a corner and wail, "Poor little me!"'

'No way,' she said with a shudder. 'It's just that I'm not used to this "eye for an eye" business.'

'Don't worry. You've made an impressive start.'

'How did you come to be there at that moment?'

As soon as the words were out she recalled, too late, that he visited his wife's tomb every night.

'It was pure chance,' he said briefly. 'I was taking the air. I'm glad it happened. Your conversation with your enemy was most illuminating. Don't waste any tears on him, or anyone. It's best if you get used to it. You'll be safer that way.'

'Don't you ever forgive your enemies?'

'Never,' he said simply. 'My enemy is my enemy for life. *Basta!* Once I know that, I would have no compunction about what I did.'

'But that's dangerous. What about the innocent who get caught in the crossfire?'

It was a remark at random, but it produced an astonishing effect on him. He backed off as though she'd struck him and his face grew visibly paler.

'*Mio dio*,' he whispered softly. 'You know where to aim your stiletto. Do your eyes see every secret I have?'

'No,' she said, puzzled. 'I can't see your secrets. I'm not

trying to pry. I only meant that you can't simply give ven-geance a free rein. It would be too cruel.'

'This from a woman who's just sent her lover out in the wilderness on a fruitless search.'

'He deserved it. But I'd back off before hurting someone else.'

'Then you're different from most women who don't care who they hurt.'

He saw her regarding him with a frown, and said quickly,

'Perhaps it's time to go to bed. I think we've both had enough for one evening.'

'Yes. Goodnight.'

It was a relief to be alone. As she climbed the stairs, hearing her own footsteps echoing on the marble floor, she knew that something had happened tonight, something she needed time to think about.

Matteo's voice was echoing in her head.

'We all believe that we have only to smile, to utter words of love, and the woman falls under our spell. The truth, of course, is that she despises us.'

In a blaze of illumination, she realised whom he had been speaking of.

It was his dead wife.

Holly had soon discovered that Liza was good at drawing, and the two of them spent happy times together with pencils and sketchbook. It was a pleasure to teach a child who learned so quickly, but sometimes she stepped back and gave Liza her own space, interested to see what she would produce. The results were revealing.

Liza had a gift for figures, and after a while Holly realised that Liza was producing the same picture over and over. It showed a happy family consisting of a mother, a father and a little girl. Sometimes the mother and child were shown together, sometimes the father and child. But she never drew the parents alone together.

Of course, she wouldn't know how they looked when she wasn't there, Holly reasoned. But still, this reticence struck her as strange. When she ventured to mention it Liza didn't reply but her face held a withdrawn look, such as Holly sometimes saw on her father's.

There were other things to puzzle her. Although sometimes Matteo almost seemed to avoid his daughter, she was often aware of him walking in the garden, not approaching them, but watching them from a distance. Once she tried to beckon him forward, hurrying through the trees to where she thought he was standing, but she was only in time to see him disappearing in the distance.

The hardest thing of all was that, on her return, Liza asked eagerly, 'Was that Poppa?'

'No, there was nobody there,' she said quickly, unable to tell Liza that he had avoided them.

One morning a parcel arrived for her. Puzzled and intrigued, she pulled it open, and stared.

It was the black cocktail dress that had tempted her before she forced herself to be sensible. And beneath it was the dark crimson dress—'the second part of your order' as a paper proclaimed.

She hadn't asked for them, she thought wildly. Then how…?

Then she remembered Matteo walking behind her at the crucial moment. He had seen everything and added them to the order later.

Just then he came in and glanced at what she was doing.

'I'm glad they've arrived,' he said.

'You shouldn't have ordered these without telling me,' she reproved him, but not very seriously.

'You're free to send them back.'

'Well—I may do that,' she said, knowing that she didn't sound very convinced.

'I'm giving a dinner party tomorrow evening. My friends are fond of Liza, so I'd like you to bring her down. I'll send a message when I'm ready.'

At that moment Liza put her head around the door.

'There you are,' she said. 'I've got the book. You promised to read it to me.' To her father she explained, 'It's in English. Holly reads it to me in English, but she stops when it gets exciting, so I have to read some myself to find out what happens next.'

To Holly's surprise a wintry look suddenly crossed his face.

'Yes, that's an excellent way to learn a language,' he murmured. 'I must be going. Don't forget what I said about tomorrow.'

'We're going downstairs to meet your Poppa's guests,' Holly explained in response to Liza's curious look.

Liza made a sound of delight and tried to seize her father's arm, but he removed himself at once.

'I must get to work,' he said at once.

'Oh, please, Poppa, just a few minutes.'

'I'm busy, *piccina*,' he said gruffly. 'No, let me go.'

Holly moved the child gently away, smiling to distract her from her father's evident eagerness to escape. He took endless trouble for her, yet again and again Holly sensed him seeking to put a distance between them.

'Is it the procession today, Poppa?' Liza asked.

'No, tomorrow. That's why some of them will be joining

me for dinner, as they do every year. And you will meet them, *piccina,* so you must be on your best behaviour.'

'Yes, Poppa.'

Liza spoke docilely, but it was as though a cloud had fallen over her. Holly was angry with him. All his child wanted was a little of his attention, and the best he could manage was a command to be on her best behaviour.

At that moment she could gladly have throttled him.

What hurt even more was that when she looked at Liza the child had assumed a bright smile, heartbreaking in its refusal to admit defeat.

'What's this procession?' Holly asked.

Liza's brow furrowed as she tried to explain.

'It's all about lawyers—and courts—and—and the judges walk in a procession from the town hall to—well, anyway, they have a procession. We can watch it on television.'

That was all she knew, and Holly had to curb her impatience until next morning. It was her first sight of Matteo in his official black robes, with the long gold tassels on the shoulder.

'It's only judges who have gold tassels,' Liza said. 'Ordinary lawyers have silver.'

The way she said 'ordinary lawyers' told volumes about her feelings for her father. She might only be a child, but her eyes shone with pride and admiration as she watched him walk with the other judges, putting them all to shame with his height and good looks.

'That's Judge Lionello,' Liza said, pointing to the plump, smiling man beside her father. He looked about sixty, with sharp eyes and gleaming silver hair.

'He's ever so nice,' she continued. 'Poppa calls him his mentor, but I don't know what that is.'

'A mentor is someone who tells you how to do things.'

'Nobody tells Poppa how to do things,' Liza said wisely. 'He won't allow it.'

'I can imagine.'

The procession came to a brief halt, and the camera lingered on Matteo. Holly realised that he was younger than the other judges, and somehow more sharply defined, as though nature had designed him to stand out from any crowd. In the set of his head there was a pride that would always have given him authority, no matter where or when.

His only flaw, she decided, was his looks. He was far too handsome to be a judge. It was a positive incitement to disrespect the law.

As she watched, he turned to Judge Lionello at his side, and gave him a smile that made Holly catch her breath. It was a smile such as she had never seen from him before—warm, affectionate, generous. For a moment all the barriers he normally kept tightly in place were abandoned, revealing the attractive man underneath.

That's what he's really like, she thought. But he keeps it a secret because he doesn't trust anyone, except another judge.

However, along with her reluctant admiration came a sense of antagonism that she couldn't understand. She owed him everything, starting with her safety and reaching as far as the soft garments that touched her body intimately. And yet—and yet the hostility was there, puzzling, confusing, but undeniable.

Matteo's smile faded as the procession moved off again. But she had seen something that she would not forget.

That evening she and Liza watched together from an upper window as the long black limousines arrived for the dinner. There was a small sprinkling of women but this was a largely male gathering.

Tonight Liza was allowed out of the wheelchair, and was full of excitement, dressed in a pretty blue dress that came down to her feet to hide her damaged leg.

For her own garments Holly had resisted the cocktail dresses and chosen a pair of smart dark blue trousers and a white silk top. Her hair had been washed and brushed until it shone, and when Matteo sent for them to join the party she hoped she looked a suitable combination of elegance and restraint.

He introduced her as a family connection of his wife, which produced a stream of cordial acknowledgements. Everyone greeted Liza with delight, and it was clear that she was a general favourite, at home in this company. After the first few minutes of keeping a wary eye on her Holly was able to relax.

'Please, allow me to get you a glass of wine,' said one very good-looking young man. 'And then we will talk in English, because I am most anxious to improve my foreign languages, as a good lawyer must.'

Since his English was already perfect this was obviously the advance of a practised flirt. But as he was genuinely charming she laughed and accepted a glass of wine.

'My name is Tomaso Bandini,' he said with a little bow. 'And I think we are going to be great friends.'

'Not if you get me into trouble with my employer,' she pointed out. 'I'm here to look after Liza.'

'But Liza is enjoying having a fuss made of her by Signor and Signora Lionello. So you are free to enjoy me making a fuss of you.'

He didn't get the chance. Several of the other men were regarding Holly with admiration. It took all her tact to escape politely, and she might not have managed it if Matteo had not come to her rescue, easing her away from the crowd.

'Thank you,' she said. 'I don't quite know what happened there—'

'I think I can make a moderately successful guess at what happened,' he said drily. 'I think Liza should go to bed now.'

The goodnights took some time, since everyone wanted another word with Liza, and several of the men insisted on a final goodbye with Holly.

'Behave yourself, Tomaso,' Matteo ordered with grim good humour.

'I was only—'

'I know what you were *only*. Now, let go of Holly's hand. She may have some other use for it.'

'She has indeed,' Judge Lionello announced, seizing her hand in his turn and kissing it with such respect that she could not object.

'You should be ashamed at your age,' Matteo told him.

'I am. Deeply ashamed. Signorina Holly, you must visit the court and let me show you around. Shall we say—?'

'Shall we say that it's time for my daughter to go to bed?' Matteo asked.

Judge Lionello sighed and relinquished his prize. But he winked at her first. She backed off quickly, conscious of his wife's eyes on her, and feeling sorry for the older woman.

Upstairs Berta had just arrived back after a day spent choosing her trousseau, and helped Holly undress the child. As she snuggled down, Liza was trying to stay awake, but her eyes were closing despite herself.

'It was a lovely party,' she whispered.

'Yes, wasn't it?'

'Did you have a good time, Holly?'

'I had a wonderful time. Go to sleep now.'

She dropped a kiss on Liza's forehead, then watched with

pleasure as the child snuggled down, asleep. Then she went to the window and looked down, smiling as she remembered Tomaso and his silly jokes. She was in no danger of falling for him, but he was diverting company.

'*Bella* Holly.'

The voice floated up to her from below. Looking down she saw Tomaso standing there, raising his glass to her.

'*La mia piu bella Holly,*' he sighed.

'I am not *your* Holly,' she told him, smiling.

'No, you are no man's. You stay up there, remote, out of reach like the sun and the moon, while below your slave yearns for you.'

'Behave yourself,' she chuckled.

'Ah, you cut me to the heart. My passion is rejected.'

'Your passion comes out of that wine glass.'

His response to this was to smite his forehead and wail in abandon. The sound brought other guests out to discover what was going on. When they saw Holly the men also saluted her with their glasses.

'You abandoned us,' one of them called out.

'We are desolate,' cried another.

Matteo appeared from the house, glancing up, eye-brows raised.

'Has Berta returned yet?' he called.

'Yes, she's here with Holly.'

'Then come down and join us.' When she hesitated he added, 'A good host always fulfils his guests' wishes. Please come down now.'

'Go on,' Berta urged. 'I'll stay here with Liza.'

Laughing, she went downstairs. Matteo met her at the door to the garden and she said reassuringly, 'I'll only stay for a moment.'

'You'll stay as long as we all want you,' he said, grinning.

'But aren't you going to discuss serious legal business?'

'Not after the second bottle, I promise you. I will only say, beware of Tomaso, who is young and enthusiastic about too many things at once.'

'That's rather what I thought.'

'And beware my old friend Andrea Lionello, who ought to have learned better long ago. But most of all, beware Signora Lionello, who has murder in her heart.'

'Well, she has all my sympathy, being married to that old rip.'

'Don't let her suspect your pity, whatever you do. That really would make her take out her stiletto.'

'Thank you for the warning.'

Holly was the hit of the party. By accepting only one glass of wine, and sticking to that, she managed to stay clear-headed enough to see the curious glances at Matteo from people who wondered what he was really up to. But after a while she forgot him in the heady pleasure of being a social success for the first time in her life.

There was no more to it than that, since she didn't take any of this seriously. It was merely an extension of the new woman she was becoming. The provocative underwear, her decisive encounter with Bruno, the heady discovery that she was strong enough to dismiss him…all these were steps along the path that led to this moment. For the first time men sighed over her and kissed her hands while their eyes swore eternal, if untruthful, vows. It had never happened before and she was going to enjoy making up for lost time.

She gracefully declined to flirt with Lionello. He was charming but she didn't rate charm as highly as she once had, and she suspected that his wife had much to put up with. Signora Lionello ostentatiously ignored her.

'No, I won't drink any more,' she said at last, laughing but firm. 'I don't trust a word from any of you.'

This produced cheers. Behind her somebody asked, 'I wonder who you distrust the most.'

With no idea who had spoken, she flirtatiously retorted, 'Why, you, of course,' turning with a teasing smile, which faded when she saw who it was.

'I've always known that you didn't trust me,' Matteo observed, amused.

'Well, as long as it's mutual,' she said lightly, recovering herself.

'I promise you it is,' he returned in the same tone. 'Although I recall that we did once form a brief alliance—'

'Of course.' She laughed into his face. 'My enemy's enemy is my friend. But when my enemy is off the scene—'

'Then all things must be reconsidered,' he agreed. 'I would only warn you against being too sure that your enemy really is off the scene. Some of them have an infernal habit of reappearing.'

'You think—?'

'I think only that a little caution is called for. And if the moment should come,' he shrugged, 'I shall still be here for you to make use of me.'

He inclined his head in a brief bow and moved away, leaving her to reflect on his strange choice of words.

Holly lingered a while longer, but was clever enough to leave soon, to a chorus of disappointment.

'There is no need for you to go,' Matteo said quietly. 'You are welcome to remain if you wish.'

'Thank you, but I choose to leave. I really don't belong here.'

'Surely that is for me to say?'

'You don't need to say it. We both know it's true. Good-night, *signore*.'

CHAPTER SEVEN

FROM her window above Holly listened to the murmurs as the party drew to its close. She heard the cars as they departed, then the silence.

She should undress and go to bed, but until she did so the most exciting night of her life hadn't officially ended. She was still restless and the moonlit grounds were very tempting. Going quietly downstairs, she slipped out of the back door, down one of the paths, into the shadows.

So many unanswered questions, so much confusion. Her life was like the paths briefly lit by the moon before winding into the darkness to an uncertain destination. Tonight that uncertainty had taken on a new and brighter aspect. The admiration that had flowed over her was such a pleasant experience that even confusion was of the cheerful kind.

She couldn't help smiling at some of the things that had been said to her, and the many significant glances she'd been given. And not only from the guests. If she was honest, it was Matteo who had chiefly caught her attention. His looks, his voice, the admiration in his eyes. She'd seen it all, and now she had time to brood about it.

Looking back at the house, she saw that most of the windows had darkened, and realised how late it was. Time to go in. She took the quickest route that lay past the judge's office. One of the French doors was slightly ajar, and she turned aside, meaning to pass it quickly. But she was stopped by the sound of a voice filled with malice and dislike.

'You saw how she acted tonight, flaunting herself before the men.'

'She was there because I invited her,' Matteo replied.

The woman's answer was a snort of contempt, and now Holly recognised her voice as belonging to Signora Lionello. Having concealed her feelings for most of the evening, she was giving them full expression now.

'And didn't she make the most of it! I don't know what wiles she used to worm her way in here, but a creature like that—'

'Like what? You don't know her.'

'I know her kind, a common little baggage who'll use her position here to get a rich boyfriend, or even husband. Then she'll walk out and leave Liza weeping. You should get rid of her before any damage is done.'

Holly knew she should walk away. Eavesdropping was disgraceful behaviour. But no power on earth could have made her leave without hearing what Matteo would say about her. She would just have to resign herself to being disgraceful.

Matteo sounded as though he was maintaining his good temper with an effort.

'I know that Andrea isn't the most perfect of husbands, but he's had a roving eye for years, not just tonight. It's unjust to blame Signorina Holly for what was not her fault.'

'She'll be setting her cap at you next.'

'I doubt it. In any case, my heart is armoured and nothing will change that. She's here for Liza's sake, and for no other reason. Believe me, I know what the problems are, and I know how to take care of them.'

From where she stood Holly could clearly see him. She saw, too, the moment when he raised his head and nodded as if he'd come to a decision.

'And just how are you going to take care of them?' she murmured.

She moved softly away, curious but not alarmed. These days she was beginning to feel that nothing could scare her any more.

To her relief she heard nothing from Lionello, but two days later Tomaso Bandini called and invited her out.

'Don't even think of it,' Matteo said when she told him. 'He's too "unfinished" for you.'

'I disagree. It sounds fun. I haven't been to Rome yet and it's time I went.'

'Of course. You're entitled to some enjoyment. I shall arrange it.'

'Oh, really!' she exclaimed, torn between antagonism and something that was suspiciously like delight. 'You're so organised! You plan this, you plan that—'

'And I shall plan a pleasant evening out for you. As you so rightly remark, I'm good at arranging things.'

There was something in his manner that might almost have been humour. It was hard to be sure.

Holly decided to accept Tomaso's invitation anyway, and wrote him a note saying so. He wrote back saying that he was devastated to be unable to make good his promise, but a sudden increase of work had made it necessary etc. etc.

She had no difficulty in seeing Matteo's hand behind this, and it made her relish the next stage of the battle even more. Squaring up to Matteo was becoming a pleasure in its own right.

She heard the opening shots being fired when he informed her at breakfast the next morning that his car would call for

her that evening at eight o'clock. She was about to protest at
this way of taking her consent for granted when he leaned
towards Liza, saying conspiratorially, 'I'm showing Holly
some of the city tonight, if you agree.'

'I'm sure Liza would prefer that I remain with her,' Holly said.

'But you never enjoy yourself,' Liza protested. 'You
should go out.'

Having been outwitted, Holly gave up and merely asked,
'Where are we going?'

'You'll see when we get there. But wear your black dress.'

She didn't even bother to argue. Besides, she was secretly
longing to wear the black dress.

Holly knew she was right when she saw herself in it that
evening. Its slinky seductiveness suited her slim figure,
making her feel good about herself as nothing had ever done
before. Her make-up was discreet. She needed little artificial
help tonight. Her whole being glowed.

Carlo, the chauffeur, was ready on the dot, and handed her
into the sleek black car. As they sped into Rome he said, 'You
enjoy the opera, *signorina*?'

'We're going to an opera house?'

'In a sense. The judge is waiting for you at the Caracalla
Baths.'

'Baths?' she echoed cautiously.

'The Emperor Caracalla built a public bath complex nearly
two thousand years ago. It's a ruin now, but every summer
there are performances of operas.'

The light was fading fast by the time they entered the
city, and her first view of the huge stone ruin was in flood-
light. Before she had finished gazing with delight she saw
Matteo, tall and elegant, standing by the kerb, waiting for
her. He was in a dinner jacket and black bow-tie, and even

in the crowds that thronged the streets he stood out as an impressive man.

'Take the rest of the night off,' he told the chauffeur as he handed Holly from the car.

Close by was a small bar, and he led her inside. 'We have time for a drink before the performance.'

As she seated herself she was aware of him studying her with approval.

'I see you resisted the temptation to send that dress back,' he said. 'I'm glad. I thought at the time that the black would suit you better than the red.'

'At the time? You mean, on that first evening? Just how far ahead have you been planning?'

He shrugged lightly. 'No good lawyer allows himself to be outwitted by unforeseen events.'

'So when I turned up in your compartment on the train, you had anticipated everything?'

'Well—perhaps not quite everything,' he conceded, smiling at her.

She smiled back, enjoying the shared joke. But at once she wished she hadn't. It simply wasn't safe to laugh with this man and risk something irresistible coming into his eyes, with double the force as they met hers directly.

Holly had a sudden mischievous urge to ask just how far ahead he had organised her life, and whether she would be allowed any say in it at all, but wisdom made her suppress it. They had a distance to travel yet and there would be time enough to tease him.

'Which opera are we going to see?' she asked, changing the subject to something safer.

'It's a concert tonight. I think you'll enjoy it. It starts at nine o'clock, so we should be going soon.'

Her first close look at the Caracalla Baths astonished her.

'I thought it would be a sort of swimming pool,' she said, looking around at the open-air theatre under the stars, the huge stage, flanked by two great, ancient brick columns.

'It was a lot more than a swimming pool,' he said, enjoying her awe. 'There was a gymnasium, a sauna, a hot bath, a warm bath and a freezing bath. After that you got to swim in the pool, browse in the library or wander the grounds. Now all that's left is a ruin—'

'But what a ruin,' she said, turning right round, and then again. 'And all the grandees used to bathe here?'

'Not just grandees. There would be nearly two thousand at a time. This place was for everyone. We Romans do things properly.'

'We Romans,' she said with a hint of teasing. 'You make it sound as thought it's all still happening.'

'But it is,' he said. 'Look around you.'

She did so, and saw how the crowds were pouring in, how the lights made the ruins vivid. After nearly two thousand years this place was alive in a way that many new buildings would never be.

And so was the man looking at her with a vibrant intensity that she couldn't dismiss. He threw everything else into shadow, and made her conscious of each part of herself, responding to him.

The concert was a selection of light music, popular arias, bouncy overtures and Strauss waltzes. As the music washed over her, filling her with ease, Holly knew that Matteo had chosen perfectly. It was like being caught up in a delightful dream of which he was a cleverly unobtrusive part. She could sink into it or emerge from it, as she pleased.

Now, she felt, she understood his plan. He was trying to

enchant her, even to make her fall a little in love with him—
and all to keep her reserved for himself and Liza.

But she knew he had no idea of loving her in return. She
had heard him say, 'My heart is armoured, and nothing will
change that.' This was merely to keep her away from the at-
tentions of other men. He would coax her just so far into love,
then say, Stay there! as he might to an obedient dog.

Cheeky, she thought, more amused than annoyed. But at
least I know what you're up to, so there's no harm done. And
I've discovered that I can play games, too.

'Why are you smiling?' he asked her as the applause died
away.

'Was I? I didn't know.'

'That makes it even more intriguing. You were wrapped up
in some private thought of your own; one that fascinates you.
Perhaps you are plotting something?'

He paused, but she stayed silent, merely turning her smile
directly onto him.

'I see,' he murmured with a slow nod. 'You mean to pique
my curiosity.'

'What makes you think it has anything to do with you at all?'

'I hope it has.'

'Then you're very conceited. My thoughts had drifted else-
where. I apologise. Since you're entertaining me it was rude
of me to be thinking of other m—that is, of anyone...
any*thing* else.'

She thought she'd managed that rather well. He thought so
too because his eyes gleamed appreciation.

'Not Bruno,' he said. 'Only promise me that. It would dis-
appoint me to think you were yearning for that piece of trash.'

'Not Bruno, I promise. In fact, it was Tomaso.' She gave a
wistful sigh. 'I wonder how I managed to lose his interest so

quickly. But you, who are his friend, can advise me how to win back his heart.'

He raised her hand and brushed his lips against the back. 'Magnificent,' he whispered. 'Your tactics are perfect.'

'So is my strategy,' she assured him.

'Don't tell me I've met a woman who actually knows the difference between tactics and strategy?'

'Strategy is when the enemy is out of sight, and tactics are for when the enemy is right in front of you.'

'And I'm the enemy?'

'I don't know. Are you?'

'I haven't quite decided.'

Holly leaned back, regarding him with a slow, luxurious smile.

'Neither have I,' Holly assured him.

The second half featured a well-known soprano singing of love betrayed. She was a superb performer, but Holly was untouched. Heartbreak was yesterday. Today led to tomorrow—and the next day...

As they left the baths he said, 'It's only midnight. We have time for a little supper.'

He made it sound like a spontaneous decision but she wasn't surprised when they reached the restaurant to find the table booked.

He gave the order for food, then asked, 'Do you have any preferences for wine?'

'I should like to drink champagne, please. I have a special reason.'

The champagne was served at once, and when they were alone again Matteo asked, 'What are we celebrating?'

'My freedom,' she said, raising her glass with a sigh of delight. 'I wasn't sure of it until tonight, but now I am.'

'Why tonight? What is it? Holly, why are you laughing? Am I being stupid about something?'

There was an edgy note in his voice, as if she'd touched a nerve.

'Not at all,' she hastened to reassure him. 'It's just that we're here, in public. If you can risk being seen with me, then I must be safe.'

'I don't think you have anything further to worry about. Bruno is no problem as long as he makes himself scarce, which he seems to be doing. Forget him. You're here to have fun. How long since you last had any? The last time you saw him, I suppose.'

'No,' she said, suddenly realising. 'Being with Bruno was heady and thrilling, but I was too tense to simply enjoy myself. Maybe I sensed even then that something else was going on.' She gave a half-smile. 'But that's the beginning of wisdom, isn't it? Knowing that something else is always going on.'

'Perhaps not always,' he said cautiously.

'Oh, I think so. Or at least far more often than people realise, and usually with the last person you'd expect.'

'But according to you it can be expected from everyone,' he pointed out, watching her.

'I've had time to learn from experience, and it's very illuminating.'

He didn't answer at once, but she could feel the teasing humour die.

'Yes, it is,' he said heavily at last.

'I can't look back far enough to find an evening I've enjoyed like tonight. It's as if you've given me a new world. You're right. This was a wonderful idea. And practical, of course.'

He was refilling her glass but he stopped, looking up in surprise.

'Practical?'

'Certainly. We need to talk about Liza, and it's difficult at home because she's such a sharp little thing that she always knows what's going on, and wants to be part of it. So arranging to meet outside was a really clever idea on your part.'

'I see. I was as clever as that, was I?'

'Oh, yes. Of course, it helps that you're a judge—having an businesslike mind, I mean.'

He regarded her with ironic appreciation, and didn't even try to find an answer to this. One up to her, she thought.

'Now, about Liza,' she resumed. 'I think I've gone as far as I can on my own, but I need you to tell me a lot more, not just about her, but about her mother.'

'Surely you can learn that from Liza herself,' he said gruffly.

'Not really. A little girl can't know everything, even about herself. I know she's trying to see her mother in me, but sooner or later she has to let go. If she starts telling herself that Mamma has somehow come back—well, that wouldn't be good for her. I'm going carefully, feeling out each situation, one by one, but I'm groping in the dark.'

'Then you're doing something right by instinct,' he said. 'That book that you're reading together—it belonged to Carol. She used to read it to Liza. She wanted her to be fluent in her own language as well as Italian.'

'That was shrewd of her. We talk in English and Italian, and we're both improving. Sometimes I think she's teaching me more than I'm teaching her. That's good for her. It helps her self-esteem.'

He made a restless movement. 'Carol used to say exactly the same,' he said. 'It's almost eerie. You are exactly what Liza needs.'

'But she needs you much more than me—'

'She needs a mother—'

'She needs a parent,' Holly said firmly. 'Liza's lost one parent and she needs the other one more. I'm just a substitute, but you're her father. You're more necessary to her than anyone on earth.'

'You talk as though I weren't here—'

'Sometimes I think you're not—in any sense that matters. The other day she and I were in the garden, she was talking about you, and I'm sure you were there, standing close by in the bushes.'

He nodded.

'Then you must have heard what she said about you.'

'Yes,' he said quietly. 'I heard.'

'But you slipped away. I wish you hadn't. If you'd come out, and put your arms around her and told her how much you loved her—it would have meant the world to her. Why do you never do that?'

'How do you know that I *never*?' he asked sharply. 'You don't always see us together.'

'Are you any more demonstrative when I'm not there?'

'No,' he admitted. 'I'm not a demonstrative man.'

Recalling what she'd seen in the photographs, Holly didn't believe this for a moment.

'You demand a lot of understanding from an eight-year-old child,' she said with a touch of anger. 'What about what she wants? Why don't *you* try understanding *her*? She needs to be reassured about your love, all the time, every minute, every second. She needs to see you as soon as possible in the morning and last thing before she falls asleep. She needs you to put your arms around her suddenly, spontaneously. She needs to look up and find you smiling at her. You could do all this once, so why is it so hard for you? I know you adore her, everyone says so…'

His head went up.

'Everyone?' he echoed sharply. 'Who have you been talking to? Who is this "everyone" who seems to know my private business? My staff, I suppose.'

She cursed herself for being clumsy. She should have known this touchy character would resent being discussed behind his back. She tried to mitigate the damage.

'Don't blame them. They haven't been gossiping, just trying to put me in the picture, which I appreciate. They all say how much you love her, what a devoted father you've always been.'

'I'm sure they meant well,' he said in a cool voice. 'And so did you. Let us leave it there for the moment.'

'But if we could only—'

'I hadn't realised how late it was. You must be longing for your bed, and I have a heavy day tomorrow. Waiter!'

It was no use. The moment was over. The waiter called them a cab and a few minutes later they were on their way back to the villa. On the journey they talked about nothing in particular, and did it with great determination.

It was only when the cab had gone and the doors of the villa had closed behind them that he said quietly, 'I'm sorry.'

'I was clumsy—'

'No, it was my fault,' he said with a quick disclaiming gesture. 'There are things it's hard for me to speak of, or even think of, but I had no right to take it out on you.'

'Do you want to go on talking now?' she asked softly.

They were standing in the half-lit hall and his face was in shadow, but she had the sense that he was on the verge of agreeing.

'Matteo,' she said, using his name for the first time, 'can't you trust me?'

'Of course,' he said slowly. 'I do trust you—you know I do...'

He took her hand and held it in his, as though there he would find something he needed.

'Holly—' he murmured, 'Holly—if only...'

Her heart lifted at what she heard in his voice. He continued to stare down at her hand as his fingers closed slowly over it. She clasped him back, suddenly filled with delighted expectancy.

'Poppa!'

The eager voice from above made them look sharply up, while their hands slipped away from each other.

'Poppa!' Liza stood on the landing, trembling with eagerness. 'I thought you weren't coming home.'

She began to stump down the stairs, awkward on her bad leg. Matteo muttered something, rushing up to help her so that she fell into his outstretched arms.

'What are you doing up at this hour?' he chided gently. 'You should be in bed and asleep.'

'I was watching for you and Holly.'

'I'm here,' Holly said, starting to climb the stairs.

'Oh, good,' the little girl said.

She was snuggled contentedly in her father's arms and Holly sent up a silent prayer of gratitude that this had happened now, reinforcing what she had been trying to tell him. Surely he must see how his daughter loved and needed him?

But as Liza buried her face against him, and he held her, he was staring into the distance, and Holly thought she had never seen so much despair in one man's face.

CHAPTER EIGHT

MATTEO might resist everything Holly was trying to tell him, but she had her first sign that he was listening to her next morning when he knocked on Liza's door, calling, 'Are you up yet?'

Liza's shriek of delight was answer enough. When Holly opened the door to him Liza held out her arms so that he could lift her and set her down in the wheelchair, which he took downstairs himself. After that breakfast was a happy meal, and before he left for work Matteo glanced at Holly with a question in his eyes, almost as if seeking her approval.

Later that day he called her.

'We might try again,' he said, 'and see if we manage better this time.'

Her heart leapt, and it was only then that she understood how dull the world would have been without the prospect of going out with him again.

Instead of sending a driver he collected her himself and drove to a small, discreet restaurant set on a hill, from which they could look across and see Rome in the distance. The view was magical; the faint glitter of the River Tiber, the floodlit dome of St Peter's floating in the distance.

This time they avoided dangerous subjects, enjoying the

meal and talking on the light level of people who had nothing else to think of.

'Another coffee?' he asked at last.

'Yes, please, I…' She broke off, seeing that she had lost his attention, and looking at the man who'd raised his hand to Matteo. Then alarm seized her.

'Police!'

'Not to worry,' he said reassuringly. 'That's Pietro, whom I know well because he used to be my bodyguard. Good, he's turning away, too tactful to disturb us.'

When the uniformed man had moved off she said, 'Bodyguard?'

'A couple of years ago I presided over the trial of a man called Fortese. He was a nasty character who uttered a lot of threats. So I had police protection for a while, but then the trial ended, I gave him thirty years and he's been locked away ever since.'

'He threatened to kill you?' she demanded, aghast.

He gave one of his rare grins. 'I suppose he thought it was a better bet than a long sentence. Forget it. It happens all the time. We're a very dramatic people, as you may have noticed. We scream threats, but nothing happens.'

Holly sat sipping coffee, feeling the world change shape around her. Since she had come to Italy everything seemed tinged with danger, of one kind or another, and now here was a new kind. How sedate England seemed by comparison.

The wisest thing would be to go home, but she had no desire to do so. She was living with an intensity she'd never known before, and part of that excitement was the man sitting here, calmly shrugging aside threats against his life.

This was Italy, not merely a land of beautiful landscapes and ancient buildings, but a place where the stiletto still flashed. Here passions were violent, whether hate or love. And the strangest thing of all was that she felt at home. She had been an Italian ever since the night in the garden with Bruno, when she had discovered the joys of *vendetta*.

Matteo was watching her. 'What are you thinking?' he asked.

'Lots of things, all muddled up,' she said. 'That's how it's been ever since I came to this country. I'm even beginning to like it. Nothing here is ever quite what it seems.'

'You most of all,' he observed.

'Yes, I suppose that's true. Even I don't quite know who I am.'

'I, too, am confused about you. I didn't mean to see you again like this tonight. It might have been safer not to.'

'How do I confuse you?'

'The day we met—I saw only that you could be useful.'

'Yes,' she said, smiling, 'I realised that.'

'It's my way. I see what I want and do what is necessary to get it. It isn't an amiable trait and I tend to bulldoze my way through life. Being a judge gives me an amount of power that—' he hesitated '—probably isn't good for any man.'

'I'm not complaining,' she said. 'A bulldozer was just what I needed. Nothing else could have saved me.'

'But still,' he gave a self-deprecating smile, 'now that I've got what I wanted, I can afford to reflect that perhaps I didn't behave very well to get it.'

'That's always the best time to reflect,' she agreed, 'when you've won.'

He glanced up quickly. 'Are you making fun of me?'

'Would you mind very much if I was?'

'If it was you—no. It's just something I'm not used to.'

'I don't suppose there's been much laughter in your life recently, has there?' she asked gently.

'No, but then there never has been. I'm not a man noted for my sense of humour, as you may have observed. When people laugh I always wonder if they're looking at something over my shoulder, so I play safe and discourage laughter. That, too, is not a pleasant characteristic.'

There flashed across her mind the memory of the man in the photograph with his wife and child, laughing, full of joy. But that man no longer existed. 'Why are you so determined to put yourself down?' She added, 'We all have our unattractive side.'

'But in some of us it predominates,' he said, speaking seriously. 'I don't think well of myself at the moment—for reasons that I can't tell you—'

'I'm not trying to pry, but I would help you if I could.'

She spoke from her heart. Her own instincts and something in his manner told her that there was more here than simply grief at his wife's loss. He was like a man labouring under a crushing burden, lashing out at one moment, but reaching out for help the next. She wanted to take him in her arms and ease his pain. It took an effort not to touch him.

'One day,' he said at last, 'there are many things I would like to tell you.'

'Yes,' she said, 'yes…'

But the mood was dispelled by the approach of the waiter with more coffee. She forced herself to smile and seem normal but it was hard when she had seemed to be drawing closer to him.

He too had assumed an air of normality, saying, 'Last night we celebrated your freedom. What are you going to do with it?'

'I'm going to use it to stay here. I've no reason to hurry back to England. No close family. No job. Nobody who needs me as Liza does.' She gave a little laugh. 'I think that's my weakness—I enjoy being needed. It's *my* need, someone who depends on me, as my mother did.'

He nodded slowly. 'You were made to be needed. You

have a strength that will always draw others to you. I didn't see it at first because when we met it was you who needed help, but Liza saw something in you that would sustain her through the dark times.'

'I still wish I knew more about your wife—of course, I understand why you don't want to talk about her—'

'I wonder if you do.'

'Eight months isn't very long, and you're still grieving—'

'Are you still grieving for Bruno Vanelli?'

She thought for a moment before saying, 'Only for the person I thought he was. Remember how we talked about this once before? You were right. The happiness I knew with him is something I'll never know again. But that happiness is dead, just as the man I believed in is dead.'

'Fool's paradise,' he said sombrely. 'How long it lasts is the luck of the draw.'

'I suppose it can only be fleeting,' she said with a little sigh.

'No, it can last for years.'

'Did yours last for years?' she asked.

For a moment she thought she'd gone too far, trespassing on his private feelings. But instead of being annoyed he nodded silently.

'So you want to know more about my wife?'

'I need to know the things Liza knows—like, how did you meet?' she asked bravely.

'She was over here on holiday, being taken on a conducted tour of the law courts. She came into the court where I was prosecuting a case, and as soon as I saw her it was all up with me. I fumbled, made a fool of myself, lost the case.

'Afterwards I caught up with her before she left the court-house. She laughed at me. I was dazzled. That very night I determined to marry her. I was in love in the way the songs describe. We were married the following month. Liza was born a few months later, and I thought I was the happiest man in creation.'

'You never wanted more children?'

'Yes, but it didn't happen. She miscarried the next baby, and suffered so much that I never asked her to try again. Besides, we had Liza.'

His voice softened and he smiled as though he couldn't help himself. There it was, she thought; the thing she'd been looking for, the overwhelming love of a father for his child.

'I'll bet she was a gorgeous baby,' she encouraged him.

His answer was a grin, open and unselfconscious.

'She was the best,' he said simply. 'No other baby was like her. She did everything before other children, she walked, she talked, she smiled at everyone because she wanted the whole world to be her friend. But she smiled at me before anyone else, even her mother. If only you could have seen how she looked then—'

'But I have,' Holly told him. 'There's a book of photographs that Liza showed me, with some lovely pictures of the three of you. You seemed such a happy family.'

'We were,' he murmured softly.

'I even felt envious because I never knew my father. I'd have loved to have pictures like that, with his arms about me, looking at me with such love and pride. It would have been something to keep, even when he wasn't there any more. When you have a memory like that, it's like being blessed forever.'

He didn't answer. He seemed lost in a dream.

'Don't you ever look at those pictures?' she asked.

'No,' he said flatly.

'Perhaps you should—to remind yourself—'

'And if I don't want to remember?' he asked quietly.

'What can I say? I have no right to give you any advice.'

He managed a bleak smile. 'That never stopped any woman yet. Besides, I've made you part of it, so go ahead. Let me hear your advice.'

'You both loved Carol, and you're both grieving for her. But do it together. Talk about how wonderful she was.'

'Wonderful—'

'Well, wasn't she? You said she was dazzling when you first met, but wasn't it more than that, all the years you were together? Isn't that why you're grieving for her, because she was wonderful? Maybe you don't want to dwell on that part, but I don't think you can get through it without remembering, and sharing it with Liza. You're the only person who can do that for her.'

'I know I am,' he said heavily. 'That's the devil of it. But you don't know what you're asking. If I could talk to anyone it would be you. I'm like Liza in that. We both lean on you. It's the effect you have. But even with you...'

His voice faded and the hand that was holding hers clenched convulsively.

'It's all right,' she said. 'It's all right.'

She wasn't sure that he'd heard, but the grip on her hand remained tight. After a while he looked up, meeting her eyes, his own full of an unmistakable message. Every nerve told her that she should draw back, be cautious, but that message mesmerised her.

She leaned forward as he reached up to touch her face, drawing his fingertips down her cheek, tracing the outline of her lips. It was the lightest touch, yet the effect was electric, shuddering through her with a brilliant excitement.

'Holly,' he whispered. 'Holly—Holly—'

It was like a lightning flash. Once before a voice had spoken her name on that caressing note, and it had all been a performance. Now another man was luring her into the same trap for his own ends, and she had nearly fallen for it.

This time she'd even known what he was doing, yet the spell had worked. She'd recovered from Bruno, but to fall in love with Matteo would finish her.

'Take me home,' she said in a hard voice.

He stared. 'Holly—'

'*I said, take me home.*'

They let themselves quietly into the house.

'Goodnight,' she said, turning towards the stairs.

'Holly, don't.' Matteo took her arm. 'You've been silent all the way home and now you're trying to run away from me. I didn't mean to offend you. One moment I thought we understood each other, but then you backed off as though I were the devil. What happened?'

'It got out of hand, didn't it?' she asked wildly.

'What do you mean?'

'The clever game you're playing. "Taking care of the problems".'

'What does that mean?'

'Have you forgotten your own words so soon? I heard you talking to Signora Lionello after the party. She said I was out to get a rich husband, and you said you'd take care of the problems. I guess this is your way of doing it.'

He swore under his breath.

'Forget that,' he begged. 'It meant nothing.'

'I know exactly what it meant. You're trying to "attach me", but only just so far, so that I'm there when needed. Just so that you have the use of me for Liza. After that I can go hang. A bit like Bruno really, except that he only wanted money. You want far more.'

'Don't dare liken me to him.'

'Why not? You're playing a cynical power game, just like him.'

'A game? You think this is a game?'

His move was too fast for her to see, and the next moment she was in his arms, feeling his lips on hers. If his fingertips had excited her, his kiss drove her wild. She tried to control the fierce feelings that threatened to overwhelm her body, but he seemed set on making her acknowledge them, moving his mouth over hers with seductive power.

'Stop this,' she managed to say.

'No,' he said fiercely against her lips. 'Not until you see sense.'

He called this seeing sense? she thought wildly as he silenced her again. There was no sense in this, no logic, no calculation, no ability even to think. There was only sensation so violent that it left her trembling, and anger at the way he thought he could set her objections aside, as though they counted for nothing.

But the real treachery was the way rage became confused with desire. It was as though she had turned against herself, betraying her own resolve with the need to kiss him back, press herself against him, demand that he explore her further.

Her mouth opened against his in what should have been a protest but emerged as a sigh, encouraging him to thrust his advantage home. The feel of him caressing her with skill and purpose almost sent her wild.

She knew she must free herself from his hold, but it was hard when all her senses were betraying her. They wanted to cling to him, inviting him on to the next step, and the next, wherever the path might lead. But she would fight them, though it broke her heart.

Holly could feel him moving, drawing her back into the shadows under the stairs, but she knew that if she yielded she was lost. This time she was going to be no man's pawn.

She tried to pull herself away from him, but succeeded only in freeing her mouth.

'Let me go, right now,' she gasped. 'I'm warning you—I'm dangerous—'

She had the feeling that he was almost in a trance, but this seemed to get through to him, and his hands fell away from her so suddenly that she had to clutch the wall.

'Yes, you are,' he murmured. 'I shouldn't have forgotten that.'

She backed away until she reached a door, then turned and went through it without bothering where it led. She found herself in the dining room with its great window doors that led into the garden, and pulled them open, running outside, taking deep breaths, struggling to calm down.

Holly had promised herself that this wouldn't happen. Maybe she'd been warning herself about it from the moment she met Matteo, knowing even then that he was a man who threw Bruno into the shade. And every warning had been useless.

She walked anywhere as long as it was away from the house, away from him. As she did so, she talked to herself.

'Leave this place. Get as far away as you can. Get away from *him*.'

All useless. There was a time when she might have left this place, but it was long past.

She wandered for an hour, until at last her feet seemed to find their own way to Carol's monument. She wasn't sure why, unless she had subconsciously known that she would find him there. He was sitting on the edge of the fountain, dipping his hands into the water, throwing it over his face.

He'd discarded his jacket, and the thin material of his shirt was soaked, showing her the outline of his body beneath.

She didn't want to look at him. The passion of desire he'd roused in her could only become a greater torment with that incitement.

He looked up at her, gasping.

'I'm sorry,' he said. 'I didn't mean anything to happen the way it has.'

'Neither did I.'

'You were partly right. It started as you said. I wanted to make sure of you, but then—things changed.' When she didn't answer he said almost angrily, 'You know they did.'

'I don't know what I know, except this—I don't want to be in the arms of a man who's dreaming of another woman.'

'What?'

'You're still in love with her. You don't want me, except in one way, and you're secretly ashamed of that. That's why you came here, isn't it? You couldn't wait to beg her forgiveness for touching me.'

He stared at her. In the silvery light she could only half see his face, glinting with droplets of water, but she could sense that he was totally thunderstruck.

Suddenly he slid down from the fountain until he was sitting on the ground below and, to her astonishment, he began to laugh. Leaning back against the marble, he shook with bitter, silent mirth.

'My God,' he murmured. 'Oh, dear, sweet heaven!'

He put his hands up to his head, covering his face, rocking back and forth, almost moaning. Her anger couldn't survive that desperate sound, like that of an animal in pain, and she went down on her knees beside him, trying to take hold of him.

'Matteo, whatever is the matter?'

He dropped his hands and looked at her. He was still making choking sounds that might have been laughter.

'What's so horribly funny?' she asked.

'Everything. Every damned thing, including your ideas about me. The grieving husband, dreaming of the woman he lost. I'll tell you the truth. The only time I dream of Carol is in my nightmares.'

'But—this thing...' She indicated the monument.

'This overblown monstrosity? I built it to hide my feelings, not reveal them. I could hardly tell the world how I really regard my wife's memory.'

'How you really...?'

The tension seemed to drain out of him.

'I hated her,' he said tiredly. 'I hated her with every fibre of my being for the vicious deception she'd practised on me for years. I hated her for not telling me the truth, and I hated her even more for finally telling it to me.'

He closed his eyes and seemed to address some dreadful inner vision.

'All those years I loved her, she filled my world. I'd have lain down my life in her service. I told you I'm not a demonstrative man, but with her I was. I held nothing back. Whatever I had or was or would ever be was hers, and she knew it. She'd known it for years, and all that time...'

He opened his eyes again and turned in her direction, so that his head lay directly against the words 'Beloved wife' carved into the marble.

'I made the foolish mistake of thinking I had everything,' he continued after a while. 'I should have understood that the man who believes that has nothing at all, that when he imagines he's walking a firm road he's actually staggering across a tightrope hung over an abyss. The abyss was always there, but I never saw it.'

'You mean she stopped loving you?'

His smile was terrible, desperate, wolfish, half-mad.

'I mean that she never did love me. Not for one second. She married me for money. She liked money a lot, and the man she really loved—an Englishman called Alec Martin—didn't have a penny. I think she decided on me when she saw the house, these grounds.

'I learned all this in the last few days before she left me. She told me—boasted of it—that she'd gone on sleeping with her lover until the night before our wedding. That's why Liza was born so quickly.'

'You mean—?'

'Yes. My little girl isn't mine at all. She'd been another man's child all the time.'

Holly drew a long breath, calling herself all kinds of a fool. This had been staring her in the face if she'd had the wit to see it.

'He went away after we married,' Matteo continued, 'and stayed away for a few years, making some money of his own, I gather. So when he came back she decided to leave me for him. I said I couldn't stop her leaving, but she wasn't taking my daughter. That's when she told me that Liza wasn't mine, but Martin's.

'A few hours after they left I got a call from the hospital. The train had crashed, Carol was dead and Liza was seriously injured. I learned later that Martin had been killed too, but nobody else knew that he had any connection with us. The world only knows that my wife and child were taking a journey and their train crashed. All the rest—' he paused for a moment before resuming with difficulty '—is known only to me.'

'And Liza,' she said, horrified, 'all those years—it's in-credible—but perhaps it isn't true. Maybe Carol only said that to hurt you—'

She stopped because he'd held up a hand, shaking his head.

'I thought of that,' he said. 'When she was in the hospital I had a test done anonymously. What my wife told me was true. Liza is not my daughter. I have to accept that.'

He was silent for a while, and Holly could think of nothing to say that wouldn't have sounded inadequate. The silence hung heavy between them.

'When her condition improved,' he resumed after a while, 'I brought her home. I didn't know what else to do.'

'Does Liza have any idea?'

'None. I was afraid that Carol might have told her, but it's obvious that she still thinks I'm her father.'

'As you are in every sense that matters,' Holly said urgently. 'Hate your wife if you must but that little girl has done nothing wrong.'

'Do you think I don't know that?' he asked tiredly. 'None of it's her fault but—'

'There are no buts,' Holly insisted. 'She's the same person that she always was, a child who loves you, and who's done nothing to forfeit your love.'

He regarded her with despair.

'You're saying all the things I've said to myself a thousand times over. My head knows they're true, but that doesn't help. Logic doesn't work. Don't think I'm proud of myself, because I'm not. I do everything in my power to prevent her suspect-ing any difference, but I can't help it if the feeling isn't there.'

'Oh, goodness,' she murmured.

Matteo looked up at the sky, where the oblivious stars wheeled coldly overhead.

'She was my child,' he said. 'And then she wasn't. When I look into her face I see the face of the woman I hate, and I can't bear it.'

'Can't you try to forgive Carol?' Holly asked, realising how useless the words were even as she spoke them. It was no surprise when Matteo turned on her with real fury.

'Forgive her? Are you mad? For years she mocked me, accepting my love, luring me on to love her more, taking and taking—and all the time it was nothing but a cruel deceit while she dreamed of another man. She took and took and took, and gave nothing in return. Even my child isn't mine.

'If she'd ever been a true wife to me in her heart I might have forgiven a moment of madness—but years of cynical, cold-blooded, calculated—'

He broke off, shuddering.

'I'm sorry,' she murmured, reaching out to him.

But he flinched away from her.

'Don't touch me,' he raged. 'You, with your stupid English *reasonableness*—'

'It's got nothing to do with—'

'You're all the same. Let's tie up the loose ends and be sensible. We don't want to make a fuss, do we? *She* used to say that. It was her gift—diffusing a fuss, calming everyone down. I used to admire her for it, until now, when I realise it was a clever tactic to fool me.

'The only time she dropped it was when we made love. Then she was shrewd enough to abandon reason and drive me so wild that I couldn't think straight. That way I never became suspicious, by night or by day. Oh, she covered every angle, leaving me not one single pure and honest memory. And now you want me to forgive. Never! I thought you'd learned enough to understand about *vendetta,* but you don't know anything.'

'So you're going to teach me, are you?' she demanded, angry in her turn. 'You're going to pass on to me all the lessons you've learned about cruelty and bitterness, about being self-centred and brooding on nothing but your own wrongs to the exclusion of all else. And when I've learned that, who will look after that innocent child?'

He was silent. Her fury had taken him by surprise, shocking him into silence. Before he could recover, she jumped to her feet and walked away to the house. She had never been so enraged in her life.

Most of all she was upset with herself. She should have seen it coming. There had been brief glimpses into the depths of hell where he lived, but none of them had prepared her for the moment when rage and anguish boiled over, pitilessly exposing to her gaze everything he would have wanted to hide.

She even knew a moment of protectiveness, wanting to shield him from disclosing his vulnerability to a woman who would judge him harshly.

Then she remembered that the woman was herself.

CHAPTER NINE

WHEN Holly reached the house some instinct prevented her from going straight upstairs. She knew he would follow her, that tonight wasn't over. There were still things to be said.

She went into the library, switched on a small lamp and after a moment she heard the door open. He took a few steps into the room, then paused, standing back in the shadows, so that she could see only his outline, not his face. Even so, she could sense the uncertainty that tormented him.

'Come in,' she said, reaching for him.

She could see he was on the point of collapse and he needed comfort. He almost fell into a chair by the window.

'Forgive me,' he said quietly.

'No, forgive me. I shouldn't have gone for you like that.'

'I had no right to tell you. I promised myself that nobody else would ever find out—I don't know why I suddenly gave in—'

'Because you had to tell someone or go mad,' she said sympathetically.

He nodded, defeated.

'What about the person at the hospital who did the test?'

'He thought it was for a case. There were no names. Maybe he guessed, but he can't know.'

She thought of the terrible strain of enduring his secret

alone, letting the world think he was grieving only for his wife's death, when in truth it was the death of all hope and trust that was devouring him. How could she have missed it? Even in this light it was there, in his face the fact that he was dying inside.

'I trust you,' he said, and there was a pleading note in his voice.

'I'll never tell,' she promised at once. 'For Liza's sake—and for yours.'

'Maybe one day Liza will have to know,' he said. 'But not until she's old enough to understand, and cope. That's why I keep my distance, I'm afraid she'll detect in my manner that I feel nothing.'

'I don't believe you've stopped loving her,' Holly said fiercely. 'You can't have. It isn't possible, not if the love ever meant anything.'

'And suppose it didn't?' he asked bleakly. 'Suppose it was only my vanity, clinging to the belief that she came from our love, mine and Carol's? That's the truth about me, a weak, shallow man, who can only love a child who's an extension of himself.'

'But that *isn't* the truth about you.'

'Do you think you know me better than I know myself?' he asked bitterly.

'I know you wouldn't be suffering so much unless there were depths of feelings in you that you're afraid to admit. You say you feel nothing, I say you feel more than you can bear.'

'You don't pull any punches, do you?' he asked in a ragged voice. 'All right, tell me what to do. I'm in your hands.'

'Spend more time with Liza, just doing nothing very much. Let things happen as they will.'

He rubbed his eyes and growled, 'I suppose you're talking about—what's that fashionable phrase? Quality time—'

'No, forget quality time. What you need now is quantity time. Lots of it.'

'But—doing what?'

'Give me patience, somebody!' she begged. 'What about that swimming pool in the grounds, the one you're letting go to rack and ruin? Exercise would be good for her leg. Have the pool cleaned out and refilled, then spend the day there with Liza. Help her swim the length and back. Do it as often as she wants. But above all, be there every time she looks up. It doesn't matter whether or not you happen to be looking at her. You might even be dozing. But *be there*.'

'If you knew how busy I am—'

'I do know. And so does Liza. That's why it'll mean the world to her if you give her a whole day, not just half an hour snatched between other things, but the whole day.'

He gave a wry smile. 'You argue your case well, *avvocato*. The judge is convinced, and will obey your orders.'

'I'm not giving orders.'

He gave her a speaking look.

'I'm not,' she said defensively. 'I'm just telling you what I think will help.'

He gave a faint smile.

'The difference is hard to tell. But you're right, I'll have the pool cleaned and filled. My only condition is that you have to be there to keep a protective eye on us. I'm going to need your help, Holly. I don't know where this will lead, but I know I can't get there without you.'

'In that case, you're right to take my advice,' she said, trying to keep the atmosphere light. 'I hope you go on being wise.'

'I'm sure you'll tell me when I'm not,' he said. Suddenly he drew a sharp breath. '*Holly*—' He was shaking.

'I know, I know. It's all right—honestly,' she said,

speaking hurriedly. 'I'm going to bed now. I think you should do the same.'

She didn't feel as though she could stand any more that night.

Work began on the pool the next day. Liza was ecstatic and insisted on being there to watch everything.

Holly took a trip into Rome to buy a swimsuit for Liza, who had grown since she was last able to bathe. She also needed one herself, and lingered for a while, tempted by a bikini. But she resisted and settled for a sedate black one-piece. This was about Liza's needs, she reminded herself. And nothing else!

But the truth, as she finally admitted to herself, was that she didn't want to invite comparison with the gorgeous Carol.

The arrangement was made for two days hence. Matteo assured her that he would spend the time making certain that his desk was clear.

'And no cell phone,' Holly said.

'But I...' He met her eyes. 'Whatever you say.'

That was their only conversation during that time, as though they had made a mutual pact not to mention the events of the other night. The knowledge was there between them, but they skirted around it as if it were explosive.

Summer was drawing to its close, but it was still hot enough for an enjoyable day. Holly gave Matteo full marks for being ready in good time, showing all the signs of looking forward to a day with his daughter with eager expectation. Looking at him, standing there, smiling, his tan glowing against his white towelling robe, she knew a moment of tenderness towards him. He might be reading from her script but he was doing it with a kind of dogged desperation that touched her.

As they waited for Berta to bring Liza downstairs she jokingly ran through a check-list.

'Cell phone?'

'Left in my office.'

'Landline calls?'

'Anna has orders to take messages.'

'Visitors?'

'I'm not at home.'

'Reading matter?'

He looked startled. 'Am I allowed to read?'

'As long as it's not legal papers. A cheap thriller is best.'

'A cheap—?'

'Yes, I thought you wouldn't have anything so useful, so I bought you one when I was in Rome.' She held it up so that he could see the lurid cover and nearly laughed at his outraged expression.

'I have never in my life—'

'Then it's time you did,' she said ruthlessly. 'It'll do you a lot of good. Liza will probably doze off after lunch, and when she wakes up and sees you, you've got to be reading some relaxing rubbish. Something you can put down easily.'

'Why don't I just not pick it up?' he asked, looking over the first page with distaste.

'Do you want to do this properly, or not?'

'Nothing matters more. All right, show me the way.'

He smiled, but it was a poor effort. For him it wasn't a joke. He was following her lead because he'd run out of other options.

'Just be there,' she muttered.

'All the time. I promise.'

When Liza appeared, wheeled by Berta, he took her hand. 'Are you ready?'

Her smile and her vigorous nod of the head showed that she was approaching the peak of bliss. She began to get out of the wheelchair.

'I think you should stay there,' Holly said. 'It's quite a walk down to the pool, and you're going to need all your strength for swimming. You don't want to arrive there with an aching leg, do you?'

'All right,' Liza said equably, and seated herself with a glance up at her father, making clear that he was appointed wheelchair attendant for the day.

The four of them advanced to the far end of the grounds where the newly cleaned pool glittered in the sun.

'Isn't it lovely?' Liza cried. Turning to Holly, she said, 'Poppa built it just for me.'

'I thought this pool was built by your grandfather,' Berta said, not unkindly but with a nurse's instinct for accuracy.

Liza looked mutinous. 'Poppa built it for me,' she cried.

'But I read somewhere—'

'He built it for me,' Liza said. 'He did, he *did*!'

With ominous speed she was working up to one of her hysterical outbursts. Berta looked desperate, not knowing how to cope. Holly prepared to do her best but it was Matteo who came to the rescue.

'In a way that's true,' he said. 'My father built it, but I adapted it when Liza was younger. The shallow end was actually a metre deep, too much for a small child. I had it turned into broad steps so that she could go down gradually. That's what you were remembering, isn't it, *piccina*?'

Instantly Liza was all smiles.

'Yes, that's it, Poppa. Mamma brought me here every day to watch the workmen.' She giggled. 'She said I drove them crazy, asking questions all the time.'

Then her laughter faded and her eyes grew blank. Matteo dropped to his knees in front of her.

'Yes,' he said softly. 'I remember, she told me.'

To Holly's pleasure he put his arms about her and drew her close. She hugged him almost hard enough to choke him.

'Let's go in,' Liza cried.

The dangerous moment had passed.

Hand and hand, they went down the broad steps together. Holly dropped into the water further down and held out her arms for Liza to swim into them, which she did, supported by Matteo. Watching them, through the glare of the sun on the water, Holly could almost believe that she was seeing the picture again, the happy father and child, their love untroubled.

Liza's delight at having his full attention made her appear at her best, all sunny smiles and innocent chatter. Matteo, in his turn, seemed to relax. They made short trips into the pool, just long enough for Liza to exercise without becoming too tired. After an hour Anna appeared with a trolley bearing soft drinks and ice cream.

Liza had perfected the art of eating and chattering at the same time.

'It was Poppa who taught me to swim,' she told Holly eagerly. 'He said all the Falluccis have been brilliant swimmers, and I was going to be the best Fallucci of all.'

Holly held her breath as Liza veered dangerously close to the forbidden subject. But, although Matteo went a little pale, he smiled and said,

'So you will be, *piccina*. The best Fallucci of them all.'

As Holly had predicted, Liza spent the first hour after lunch dozing on a towel, in the shade of the trees. Matteo dived in and swam the length of the pool several times, while Holly sat, watching him vaguely, her thoughts in a tangle.

She had studied his efforts today and her heart had reached out in sympathy. Now and then Liza would say something in all innocence that must have been like twisting

a knife, but he coped. She could only imagine what it was
doing to him.

And today wasn't a real solution, she knew that.
Somewhere in the cloud of ice that had descended on his
feelings she was sure that his love for the little girl was still
there. Finding it would take time, and be painful. For the
moment he was like a lost soul, blundering about in the
darkness, but she wanted to be there with him, to help as he
struggled to find the way to go on living.

For Liza's sake, she insisted.

But she realised she wasn't being quite honest with herself.
His need was as great as the child's, and the moment when
he'd reached out to her in pain was the moment her defences
had begun to crack.

At last Matteo came up the steps of the shallow end,
pulled on a towelling robe and stretched out. He even took
out the book Holly had bought him and turned it over and
over. He read the blurb on the back page, then opened the
book and began to read, casually at first, and then with
obvious interest. He was deep in chapter one when Liza
awoke and crept over to him.

'Is it good?' she asked.

'Hm?' he answered, not lifting his head.

'Poppa!'

At last he looked at her, tearing himself from the book with
difficulty, it seemed to Holly.

'Is it good?' Liza demanded.

'Yes—yes, it's good.'

'What's it about?'

'It's about a man in prison for something he didn't do, and
planning his revenge.'

'Do you ever send innocent people to prison, Poppa?'

He looked aghast at the question. 'I try not to. I don't imprison anyone unless I think they're guilty.'

'But suppose you get it wrong?' Liza asked remorselessly.

To Holly's delight Matteo was bereft of words. He looked across at her wildly, but she was beyond being able to help. She simply lay back in the grass and chuckled.

'I'm sorry,' Holly said at last, moving over to them. 'Liza, you'll have to let this go for now. But when you're older you must become a lawyer, and then you can study your Poppa's cases and tell him where he got it wrong.'

'All right,' Liza said, satisfied.

'Thank you,' Matteo said wryly.

Having settled the future, Liza returned to the book.

'Does he do lots of horrible things to his enemies?' she demanded of her father.

'I think so. I haven't got very far in yet. I'll let you know.'

Liza gave a happy sigh.

'How can she be such a ghoul?' Matteo murmured to Holly as Berta took Liza down the steps into the pool.

'Because she's a child. Children love that kind of thing.'

'After what happened to her—'

'It's not the same. This is a book, nothing to do with reality.'

She stopped, seeing a sudden change in his expression.

'What is it?' she asked. 'You haven't really sent an innocent man to gaol, have you?'

'Not that I know of. Of course, they all protest their innocence. Sometimes the worse they are the more vehemently they protest. The worst one I ever knew was Antonio Fortese, a murderer who escaped too often.'

'Is he the one you told me about, who threatened you so that you needed a bodyguard?'

'That's right. He swore he was innocent, but he was as

guilty as hell. As you know, I gave him thirty years. He deserved every moment of it. Now he can threaten all he likes. He's locked up in a high-security gaol.'

'Maybe it wasn't very clever of me to choose that particular book.' Holly sighed.

'Why?' he asked, amused. 'Do you think it's going to give me nightmares? Forget it. Characters like Fortese are just part of the way I live. This—' he waved the novel '—is light relief.'

'Well, I'll tell you this: Liza's got a much higher opinion of you now that she knows you can get lost in a good book.'

'I won't deny that it has a certain readability.'

'That's why you didn't answer her at first, isn't it?'

Suddenly he grinned. 'Yes, I must admit I couldn't put it down.'

In this mood he was delightful, and she had to remind herself to stay cautious. There was a long way to go before there could be any true communication between them.

Anna appeared from between the trees, looking concerned.

'*Signore*, there is someone—'

'No visitors, I told you,' Matteo said.

'But *Signore*—'

Matteo looked up, irritated. Then his expression changed as he saw the elderly lady who stepped out from behind Anna.

'Mamma!'

Liza gave a little shriek and joined her father in hurrying to embrace his mother. She seemed to be in her sixties, a smiling woman of great elegance who clearly inspired affection in Matteo and Liza.

Holly watched her curiously, certain that this was no coincidence. She was even more certain a few moments later when she was called forward to be introduced, and saw the old woman look her up and down, clearly comparing her to some mental picture she already had.

'I'm sorry I didn't warn you I was coming,' she said, 'but it was an impulse.'

'You know you're always welcome,' Matteo said warmly. 'Let's go inside.'

Holly knew, from Anna, that Matteo's father was dead and his mother, Galina, had since remarried. Her husband was an invalid, and the two of them lived down south, in Sicily, where the weather suited him better. It was quite a journey to make on the spur of the moment.

'My stepdaughters came to see us,' she explained as they walked back to the house. 'They prefer having their father to themselves, so I left with a clear conscience. It's too long since I saw my favourite granddaughter.'

'I'm your only granddaughter,' Liza pointed out.

'Then you must be my favourite,' Galina returned with triumphant logic.

The rest of the day was taken up with settling her into her room and arranging the evening meal to her liking. Holly withdrew, not wanting to intrude on the family, and didn't see them again until she went downstairs for supper.

Berta was there too, and Galina greeted her as an old acquaintance. Holly said little but her mind was working furiously. Instinct told her that she was under inspection.

At any other time she would have been amused at Matteo's demeanour towards his mother, which was respectful. He might be a man of authority to the rest of the world, but he was nervous of his *mamma*. Now and then his eyes darted to Holly, as though checking whether she was making a good impression.

At last the meal was over. With relief, Holly suggested that it was time for Liza's day to end.

'Berta and I will bring her up later,' Galina said. 'Why don't you go off duty?'

It was a dismissal and she had no choice but to accept it.

Perhaps the decision had gone against her, she thought. Hence the choice of Berta. This might even be her last night in the house. It wasn't so very long ago that she had longed for the means to escape. Now she would have given anything to stay.

Just why she longed to stay was something she wasn't quite sure about yet, but it was no matter. The decision was being taken out of her hands.

At last Galina arrived with Liza, already half-asleep. Together they put the child to bed and saw her nod off at once.

'We did not mean to be so late,' Galina said softly, 'but Liza had a criminal matter she wished to discuss with her father.'

'A criminal matter?'

'Something to do with a book they were enjoying together.' Her eyes twinkled. 'Your doing, I fancy.'

'Oh, I see. Yes, it's a thriller.'

'Then it's definitely your doing. When I see my son deep in a thriller I know he's come under a new influence. Of course, I already knew that.'

'I don't understand. How could you know?'

'Because he talks of you so much. We telephone each other many times, and always he talks about you. Of course, he is very discreet, very proper. He tells me how good you are being to Liza, and how the child benefits from your care. And so I find myself curious about this wonderful person, and I decide I must meet her for myself. And now that we have met, I think I am starting to understand. I see how Liza loves you, how much good you're doing her.'

'But I wonder exactly what Matteo has told you.'

'He has told me all I need to know. If there is more—he

will tell me that too in his own good time. Let us leave it for now. I am pleased with what I find here. My son begins to look alive again and that is all I want after the way he has suffered.' She added calmly, 'Perhaps he is falling in love with you.'

'Oh, no,' Holly said quickly. 'It's much too soon for that.'

'Too soon? Why?'

'After the way he felt about her—'

'You think he still has a rose-tinted view of his wife? I don't think so.'

'Even so, it was all so terrible—he has to get over the shock,' Holly persisted.

'You're a wise woman. You will help him recover. And then—well…'

But Holly shook her head as caution swept her again.

'There's no question of it.'

'So positive? He's an attractive man with a good position in life, and you seem fond of his child. It wouldn't be impossible that you might grow to love him.'

'Yes, it would,' Holly said firmly. 'There are too many things in the way.'

'You love someone else?'

'I did once. Never again.'

'I see. Well, I'm a nosy old woman, but I won't pry any further.'

She was shrewd enough to leave it there, and over the next few days the house became a more cheerful place as her influence was felt. Emboldened, Berta gave in her notice, and departed, with a generous bonus, into Alfio's arms.

There was a small dinner party in Galina's honour, at which she kept Holly close to her, smiling contentedly in a way that made her wishes plain.

Holly tried not to spend too much time watching Matteo,

unwilling to give substance to Galina's suspicions. But her eyes strayed towards him too often for comfort, delighting not only in his looks but in his air of poise and authority, his calm detachment. He would speak to a guest, smiling enough to be polite, but the next moment he would retreat into the gentle melancholy that only she completely understood. Holly found a strange, disturbing pleasure in the thought that she knew the depths of him that were hidden from everyone else.

Yet she had no thought of marriage. Their closeness, half-sweet, half-bitter, was enough for the moment. She did not know if she should call it love. She no longer trusted herself on that subject. There was still an antagonism between them, as much on his side, she suspected, as on hers. It was nothing like the un-suspicious, uncritical joy she'd known with Bruno, but then, that hadn't been love, and she never wanted to feel it again.

Could you be in love with a man whose kisses had thrilled you to the depths one minute, and whose harshness made you want to rage at him the next?

She came out of her reverie to realise that she'd heard a faint, unfamiliar noise. One of the other men put a hand in his pocket and took out his cell phone. She saw the change come over his expression as he stared at it, evidently reading a text.

'Put the television on,' he said quickly. 'Get the news.'

In a moment they were indoors, crowded around the set, where an announcer was saying, 'Nobody knows how Fortese acquired a gun, but he used it to great effect, shooting dead two prison guards before making his escape...'

'Fortese,' Holly whispered. 'Isn't he—?'

'Yes,' Galina said, beside her. 'I have always been afraid that this would happen.' Then she forced a smile. 'But they will recapture him before he can—that is—'

'Before he can come after Matteo,' Holly said. 'Of course they'll recapture him. They must.'

'They must,' Galina agreed.

In silent dread they looked at each other.

CHAPTER TEN

EVERYTHING changed.

One moment they were enjoying a happy dinner party. The next the guests were saying goodbye, wishing Matteo good luck, but eager to get away.

Within half an hour a posse of police on motorcycles had arrived, ready to take up their positions in the judge's defence. Matteo greeted them quietly. He had shown almost no reaction to the news, merely nodding calmly as though this were a normal part of life.

And for him it was, Holly realised.

She could barely take in the way life had changed out of all recognition. It might all have been a dream, except that the swarm of armed police made it horribly real. A man who already had several murders against him had set himself to kill Matteo, and was now on the loose, with a gun.

He could be anywhere. The only certain thing was that he wanted revenge and wouldn't rest until he got it.

She went straight up to Liza's room, relieved to find her asleep. She longed to talk to Matteo, just to look at him and see him standing there alive. But protecting the child from the knowledge of what was happening had to come first.

She did not even see Matteo again that night, but the next morning he spoke to her quietly before leaving.

'Two of the police will be staying here, just in case Fortese gets ideas. All of you remain in the house and you'll be quite safe.'

He departed with barely a nod, and her last sight of him was driving away, accompanied by four police outriders.

Between them she and Galina kept Liza occupied that day, so that she should notice as little as possible out of the ordinary. It took a lot of ingenuity, especially when Matteo returned in the evening, with a change of guard. But they managed.

Galina went to his study and stayed for an hour. When she came out she said to Holly in a strangely urgent voice, 'He wants to see you.'

She found him looking pale and strained. When he spoke his voice seemed to come from a distance, which contrasted strangely with his words.

'I have to ask you a favour,' he said sharply. 'Not for myself, but for Liza.'

'Of course.'

He looked uneasy, and seemed unable to look at her as he added, 'It's something only you can do for her.'

'You know I'll do anything she needs. Name it.'

'Marry me.' It came out almost as a bark.

She frowned. She'd heard the words, but didn't divine their meaning.

'What did you say?'

'I want you to become my wife. For Liza's sake.'

Light dawned. 'Yes, I see. But there's no need—I'm not going anywhere. I've promised you I'll be here for her.'

At last he rose and faced her.

'That's not enough,' he said urgently. 'You need to be her mother—legally—so that nobody else can interfere.'

'Matteo, what are you talking about? Why should anyone interfere?'

'I mean—if I weren't here...'

Like a thunderclap his meaning burst on her.

'You mean Fortese—you actually think—?'

'If he manages to kill me Liza will need you as never before. Holly, we have to be married, so that she can't lose you as well. You're her only hope if anything happens to me.'

'Then don't take the risk,' she cried. 'Go into hiding until they catch him.'

She thought she'd never seen so much passionate outrage in one human face.

'Back off?' he said in a voice whose softness didn't disguise its vehemence. 'Let the villains win? Can't you understand that the only hope of defeating them is for people like me to face them, no matter what?'

'But you have a child—'

'We all have families, we're all afraid, but if we run away then they've won. They take over, and what happens then to all the promises we made about protecting the world from them? What happens to our children in the world that we'll bequeath them then? Holly, for the love of heaven, tell me that you understand!'

She nodded bleakly. 'I do understand.'

'If he comes after me, I'm ready for it. But what I won't do—*can't* do—is run away.' He added with an icy bleakness that matched her own, 'No matter what the cost.'

Holly tried to get away, but his hand on her arm was merciless.

'It's not like you to duck out,' he said. 'You're stronger than that.'

'I thought I was, but you're asking me to jump off a great height into the unknown. I don't know you. Much of the time I don't even like you.'

'You haven't made a secret of that. But this isn't about how we feel. It's about Liza.'

'So you said. You'll get me to do for her what *you* should do, the way you always have. It's all for Liza, because you know that's the one argument that will move me. Just like a lawyer.'

'I can't help that. I *am* a lawyer—'

'And like any good lawyer you know how to go for the jugular.'

'All right, do it for *me*,' he shouted. 'Do it so that I can sleep at night knowing I've protected her future. Do it so that I don't have nightmares thinking of her alone. That little girl has lost so much…first her mother, then her father—yes, she's lost her father. I don't mean the other one, I mean me. I try to do my duty by her, I know she's innocent, but it isn't here.' He thumped his chest with his fist. 'With your help I'm putting up a good pretence, but I can't recreate the feeling—the joy I felt at just being with her, gazing at her, knowing that she was *mine*. I can't give her the look she once saw in my eyes. I see her searching for it, puzzled that it's missing, but there's nothing I can do. Hate me for it. You can't hate me as much as I hate myself. Think as badly of me as you like, but do this for her, and for me.'

'Matteo, please—let me think, I need time—'

'There isn't any. I know it's not fair to dump this on you. What a choice to face you with!' His voice took on a note of grim humour. 'You could be a rich widow in a very short time. Or, if you get really unlucky, you might be stuck with me for years.'

'Stop it,' she said fiercely.

'I'm just trying to see it from your point of view.'

'Do you think I want to make light of it?' she demanded, beginning to be angry again. 'Is that what you think of me?'

'I'm trying to confront this the best way I can,' he said, his voice rising again in its turn, 'and you needn't tell me I'm making a mess of it, because I know that. What is the right way? Shall I go down on one knee?'

'Don't you dare!' she cried in horror. 'I'd never forgive you.'

'Then tell me how to persuade you.'

'You can't!'

'I must. You're the one person in the world that I can turn to, the only one I can rely on. You're stronger than anyone I know. In some ways you're stronger than me.'

'But to suggest that we... Why me?'

'Because there's nobody else I can trust to protect Liza.'

'Your mother—'

'She's an old lady, with a sick husband to care for. Apart from her my only family is a cousin that I can't stand. She's grim and hard, and hell will freeze over before I let Liza fall into her hands. Once you're my wife I can make sure you're her legal guardian if I'm killed.

'Do this for me, Holly, I beg you. It doesn't have to be a real marriage, just the legal formality, and I won't ask more than that.'

'Are you saying—?'

'I'll keep my distance, I swear it.'

Holly stood still, feeling herself trapped in the circle of his arms that had wound fiercely around her, almost like a steel cage. There was no escape, yet something perverse inside her persisted in fighting until the end.

'I can't—I can't—'

'You must, you must. I won't let you go until you say yes. *Holly, you have got to do this.*'

She stared fixedly into his eyes, trying to read there something that would help her. But all she could see was a terrified determination to have his own way, and she was sure of it when he played his last and most unarguable card.

'If it weren't for Liza, think where you could be now. It wasn't me who saved you. It was her, in those first few minutes on the train, telling them your name was Holly, screaming at them to go. You owe her.'

'That's a cheap shot,' she flashed.

He shrugged, half releasing her. 'Sure it is. I'll be as cheap as I have to if it makes you say yes. I warned you I'm not a nice man when I want something. Cross me and I'll fight until you give in. No holds barred.'

It was true. All his least likeable characteristics were on display because he reckoned they were his best weapons. At this moment, when he was asking her to be his wife, tossing his wealth and status into her lap, part of her disliked him as never before. The other part pitied him so that her heart ached.

And it was true. She owed the little girl everything.

'All right,' she murmured. 'For Liza.'

As soon as the words were out she was filled with misgiving. But she was committed now.

He dropped his hands, but still looked at her intently. 'You mean it? You won't go back on that?'

'I've given my word.'

Suddenly neither of them could think of anything more to say. They could only look at each other helplessly for a long moment, before opening the door, to find Galina, who'd been shamelessly listening. She was weeping with relief.

The whole household, down to the last gardener, entered into a conspiracy to prevent Liza learning about the situation.

Radio and television sets were kept switched off and no newspapers entered the house.

'All fear must be kept from her,' Galina said heavily. 'She must never know that her father's life is in danger.'

Like Matteo, Galina had accepted without question that it was her duty to carry on as normal. Holly marvelled at her courage. She wasn't so sure of her own. Already she was a part of what was happening here, caught up in a fearful dream, with no end that she could see.

'With all my heart I thank you for agreeing to become my son's wife,' Galina said to her. 'Soon I must go home to my husband. I shall feel easier in my mind, knowing that you are here to take care of Matteo.'

'I'm chiefly here to take care of Liza,' Holly said quickly.

'Yes, of course. He has explained that to me.'

'I only hope that I can do all that Matteo expects of me.'

'That depends whether you ever come to love him. You once implied that it was impossible.'

Galina's tone contained a question, but Holly had no answer to give her.

'I don't know any more now than I did then,' she sighed.

'But you said you'd marry him.'

'I had to. He wasn't going to take no for an answer.'

'That's his way,' Galina agreed. 'You will have to be strong to stand up to him.'

'He says that I am. He says in some ways I'm stronger than he is.'

'I agree. I'm glad he understands himself, and you, so well. But strength isn't enough, Holly. He will need your love. Please try to give it to him.'

She didn't wait for a reply, but plunged deep into arrangements for the wedding. One of them was overseeing the preparation of the room that had once belonged to Carol, and which had been locked ever since. In no time Galina had an army of servants cleaning it out.

Holly felt slightly uncomfortable about this, but Galina said firmly, 'You are the mistress now. You. Nobody else.'

'But Galina—'

'No ghosts,' said her future mother-in-law. 'Not in this house.'

Which left Holly wondering just how much Galina had guessed.

Matteo showed no emotion when he walked into the room and heard his mother's plans. He merely nodded, thanked her and departed.

She had feared Liza's reaction to the wedding. While part of her loved Holly, part of her still grieved for her mother, and Holly half expected her to be upset at seeing that mother supplanted. But Liza had smiled and hugged her, and Holly understood that the child had explained it all to herself in a way that satisfied her.

She was even content to see Holly move out of her room and into the one Galina prepared for her as the new mistress of the house. It satisfied her sense of what was right and proper, and strangely made her feel even safer.

'And I'm not far away,' Holly pointed out. 'Just across the corridor.'

Liza smiled, content.

A special licence was obtained for a hurried wedding, to take place in two days' time, in the private chapel at the back of the house. A few close friends were invited and everything was to be kept as secret as possible. Only Liza had any fault to find with this. She wanted to celebrate properly, and it was impossible to tell her the truth—that if the news leaked out that Judge Fallucci had married so quickly after Fortese's escape, it would be practically an announcement that he was expecting the worst.

That this was no ordinary wedding was brought home to Holly in a dozen little ways, starting with Matteo saying, 'Order your clothes online and have them delivered. On no account go into Rome.'

She didn't have to ask why. She had said she was plunging into the unknown. Now she discovered how true that was.

Another time Matteo returned her passport to her. She studied it, her familiar name, and the face that now seemed to belong to someone else.

'So now I'm me again,' she murmured. 'Whoever that is.'

The man who was to be her husband was a mystery to her. She knew that the tragedy of his marriage and his ruined fatherhood had caused him to shut down his heart. She knew him to be suspicious, harsh, exacting and alarmingly vulnerable. Beyond that she knew nothing.

Matteo spent the day before the wedding locked in his study with a civil lawyer who had brought papers for him to examine. The actual signing would take place tomorrow, immediately after the ceremony. He showed them to Holly, who saw that her legal position had been safeguarded. She was Liza's guardian and the trustee for the child's inheritance, which was two-thirds of Matteo's fortune. The other third came to herself, plus a lump sum that became hers as soon as she was his wife.

When she saw the size of that sum she stared in astonishment.

'It's only fair,' Matteo said before she could speak. 'Let's say no more about it.'

Her dress was a modest design of ivory lace, worn with a small, flowered hat. By good luck, the online store also had one small dress that exactly matched it, and Holly bought this for Liza, her bridesmaid.

The night before the wedding they were joined by his only other family members, the cousin who antagonised him and her husband. Holly disliked her on sight, and knew that it was mutual. Now she understood why Matteo was determined to keep Liza away from her, and that was a help. It enabled her to focus her whirling thoughts.

When the family was saying goodnight and mounting the stairs Matteo said quietly, 'Will you give me a few moments?' and showed her into his study.

So many times they had talked in the severe room, starting with the first night, when they had faced each other as adversaries whose mutual dependence drove them mad. Now they met for a reason that was almost as difficult.

'These are for you,' Matteo said, indicating something on his desk.

She was stunned at the sight of the three-stranded pearl necklace and matching earrings. Ignorant as she was about jewels, even she could see that these were real, and fabulously expensive.

'My wedding gift,' Matteo said.

She fingered them lovingly, awed by their beauty. But then a horrid thought struck her.

'They're not—you didn't—?'

'No, I didn't give them to Carol. I wouldn't insult you like that. Carol's jewels are locked away until I can give them to Liza. My mother chose these to go with your dress.'

If this had been a real wedding he would have chosen her gift himself. If he had loved her he would have draped the pearls around her neck and fastened them. If she had loved him she would have given him something in return. As it was—

'I haven't got anything for you,' she said. 'I'd forgotten about presents.'

'You're already giving me the only thing I want or need. No other gift could mean anything next to that. Now, it's getting late, and we should both retire. Tomorrow will be a heavy day.'

He held out the jewel box in businesslike fashion, she took it in the same way, and they bid each other goodnight.

Galina waylaid her on the stairs, full of delight, and led her into her new room.

'I had your things moved in here an hour ago,' she said. 'There won't be time tomorrow. You sleep here tonight.'

Her nightgown was laid out on the great bed. Her personal things were on the dressing table. There was nothing for her to do. In this drama she was really little more than a bit-player.

When she was alone she went around the room, trying to get her bearings. The house was several hundred years old, built at a time of greater formality. So the master and mistress occupied separate rooms, with a door connecting them. She stood before that door, trying to picture Matteo's room on the other side. There was no sound and she guessed he was still downstairs.

She undressed, turned out the light and went to the window, where the curtains were still drawn back, and sat on the window seat, watching the moonlit garden. Now and then she glanced at the slight gap beneath the door where any light would show. There was none, and she wondered what he was doing downstairs. Was he finding excuses to stay there, unwilling to come to bed?

At last she heard his outer door opening and closing. But the light didn't come on. Instead there was the sound of footsteps, then the soft click as the connecting door opened.

He had promised not to come to her, but it hadn't occurred to her to check whether that door was locked. Now she sat, frozen, as he appeared. He was in his shirtsleeves, the collar torn open.

Slowly he went to the bed and stood there, looking down. The moon, shining in, showed clearly that there was nobody there.

He didn't know she was there, Holly realised. Galina must have forgotten to tell him. He had come here because it was Carol's room.

Slowly, terrified that he would notice her, she rose and moved further back into the shadows. From here she could see the outline of his face but not his expression as he regarded the bed where he had once known such joy and such bitterness. It was impossible to tell which of the two he was remembering as his eyes were deep-sunk black hollows from which all light had vanished.

He seemed to stand there forever, motionless, as though transfixed by thoughts too sad for words. Holly held her breath, afraid that he would sense her there, perhaps because her heart was beating so loudly that he was bound to hear it.

But at last he gave a sigh, as if the strength had drained out of him, leaving him only just able to stand. Slowly he turned and walked out of the room. After a moment Holly heard the key turn in the lock on his side.

Next morning Galina and Liza helped her to dress. Then they went to the chapel, where Liza took her place as bridesmaid, and they advanced down the aisle.

When Holly saw Matteo standing by the altar, waiting for her, the mists of the dream shifted and she discovered that it was really happening.

But then another reality intruded. This was a different Matteo, ten years younger, full of love and joy as he watched his beloved approach, to become his wife. That trusting young man had believed that a life of perfect happiness was opening for him.

How much of that other wedding was he remembering?

Was he looking at her and seeing Carol, the one great love of his life, whose betrayal had ruined him for all other women? Did he regret this impulsive decision?

His face gave no clue. As she drew level he inclined his head to her, but he had no expression. His eyes, as he took her hand, were blank.

It went like clockwork. The words were spoken, the promises were given, the ties were bound. She was his wife.

No wedding would be complete without photographs, so they posed again and again, while one of Matteo's friends took the shots that were expected: the bride and groom with the groom's mother and little girl, the bride and Liza, happy together, the groom and his daughter, his mouth smiling, his eyes wary.

When it could no longer be avoided the bride and groom stood together, his arm about her shoulders. In the total un-reality of this day she found it unnerving to be pressed so close to him, smiling into his face.

But there she saw that it was the same with him. His eyes met hers and his lips moved silently saying, 'Bear up. Not long to go.'

It was only a moment, but it told her that they were on the same side, and after that it was easier.

The wedding breakfast was a sedate affair, with some short speeches, a few toasts. Then it was time for everyone to go. Watching the departure, Holly saw that the grounds were filled with unfamiliar figures and she realised that an extra contingent of police were guarding her wedding.

Finally the last guest had gone, although the officer in charge assured them that his men would remain in the grounds. Matteo thanked him formally and invited him into his study for 'further discussion'. Relieved, Holly hurried upstairs to where Galina was putting Liza to bed.

The child was slightly shocked to see her.

'You should be drinking champagne with Poppa,' she said.

'We'll do that later,' Holly said. 'Not all weddings are alike.'

'Yes, they are,' Liza insisted. 'You get married and you drink champagne, and you go away on honeymoon.'

'There wasn't time to arrange that,' Galina said hurriedly.

'Will you have one later?'

'Not for some time,' Holly said. 'Your father has a lot of work to do for the next few months.'

'But where will you go?'

'We'll talk about that another time,' Holly improvised.

Luckily this kept Liza content for the next few minutes while she went through a list of places she considered suitable. They grew crazier with every minute and the three of them were laughing when Matteo came in.

Galina immediately declared that she was ready for bed. Before departing she told Matteo, 'We were just settling your honeymoon, when you have time for it. Liza favours Timbuktu.'

To Holly's relief Matteo joined in the game, declaring that he could think of much more outrageous places. All went well until Liza said, 'I won't come in too early. Promise.'

'Come in?' Matteo echoed.

'Your room. Remember how I used to come in, in the mornings, and bring you coffee?' She gave a happy sigh. 'And you and Mamma would be all snuggled up together, cosy and warm.' She looked worried. 'Don't you remember?'

'Yes, *piccina*,' Matteo said in a voice that wasn't quite steady. 'I remember.'

'And it will be just the same, won't it?' Liza asked anxiously.

Matteo couldn't reply. Holly could feel the air vibrating with strain, and it was she who said, 'Yes, darling, it's all right. It will be exactly the same.'

CHAPTER ELEVEN

AS SOON as they were alone in her bedroom Matteo turned to face her.

'I'm sorry,' he said urgently. 'I promised to keep to my own room and I meant it. I had no idea this would happen. Holly, please say that you believe me.'

'Of course I do. I know you're a man of your word.'

'I had forgotten how Liza used to come in to see us in the mornings. I didn't know it meant that much to her.'

'But she gave you the clue,' Holly reminded him. 'She said you and Carol were "snuggled up together, cosy and warm."' She smiled. 'It made me think of a pair of cats I once had. They were elderly neuters, and they slept wrapped around each other because that way they were blissfully content. Seeing you two like that made Liza feel safe, and it's that safety she wants back.'

'Then what do we do?'

'Give her what she wants. That's what this is all about.'

'You mean we have to guess when she's going to arrive in the morning? I set an alarm clock, or do you come next door and awaken me?'

She regarded him with an exasperation that had a touch of fondness.

'I don't think that would work,' she said slowly.

They looked at each other. He spoke cautiously.

'So your suggestion is—that we spend the night like a pair of elderly neutered cats?'

'Not the whole night. Just the last half-hour. That bed must be eight feet wide. Room enough to stay clear of each other.'

He didn't speak but his eyes said, You think so, do you? And for a moment the one kiss they'd shared flamed between them. With a great effort she put it aside.

'Unless you've got a better idea,' she said.

A faint gleam of humour crept into his rueful smile.

'What must you be thinking of me?' he asked.

'That you're reacting to situations that are beyond your control, as we all are,' she said gently. 'We just have to play everything by ear and hope we get it right.'

'How will we know when we've got it right?'

'When Liza smiles, we'll know. That's what it's all about. We must never forget that.'

He nodded. After an uneasy moment he said, 'I have something to give you.'

He went into his own room and she took the opportunity to change into her nightgown, relieved that she had chosen something plain and simple, not designed to be alluring. Her dressing gown, too, was elegant but not seductive.

When he returned he, too, was wearing a dressing gown, and carrying a bottle of champagne and two glasses, which he set down on a small table.

'Take these and keep them in a safe place,' he said, reaching into a deep pocket and producing papers. 'They're your copies of the forms I signed this afternoon. Everything is now in order.'

She could see that it was. She was Signora Fallucci, now a wealthy woman in her own right and possibly heiress to a large inheritance. She was also named as the guardian of Liza Fallucci, and her joint trustee, with the lawyers, for an even larger inheritance.

Everything was provided for, down to the last comma, the work of a thorough lawyer.

But when she looked up he was holding out a fluted glass of champagne.

'We drank champagne with our guests,' he said, 'but this is between us. My gratitude—for today, and for the future.'

The future which might contain his death, perhaps very soon. Neither said it, but each knew what the other was thinking.

They clinked glasses.

'Any regrets?' he asked.

'Not yet,' she said lightly. 'I'll keep you informed. At any rate, this is nice and quiet.'

'I don't understand.'

'It's just that we seem unable to discuss anything without shouting,' she said, still in the same light tone. 'It's practically a form of communication.'

'Ah, you're talking about my proposal.'

'Yes, I suppose I am.'

'And a few other things,' he said, considering. 'I don't normally shout and get so worked up.'

'Me neither.'

'And I'm not the bully you might think from my behaviour.'

'I know. You just like to have your own way.'

'I shout when I'm scared,' he said with a shrug. 'It doesn't happen often but—well.'

She nodded.

'I'm not scared of Fortese, but when you refused to marry me—it was like trying to seize hold of something in the darkness, only the "something" kept darting away. Usually it's easy. A judge can mostly get what he wants by signing a bit of paper and letting other people do the work. But it was clear that no force was going to control you.

'Even when you seemed to be almost my prisoner I used to feel a moment of apprehension when I reached home in the evening, in case you'd mysteriously vanished during the day.'

'I never knew that.'

'I couldn't afford to let you suspect. You'd have found it too easy to run rings around me. You didn't find it very hard in any case.'

Holly stared. She had known none of this. He'd always seemed so totally dominant. Now he was revealing the weakness in his defences, and it seemed not to trouble him at all that she should know.

After a moment he went on in a reflective voice. 'I think I realised how important you were going to be from the first day. I didn't know how, but you appeared out of nowhere, and everything about you was inevitable. It almost makes me believe in fate.'

'You? A judge, believing in fate?'

'No judge is ever only a judge. He's a man too, no matter how much he might sometimes wish...' He checked himself. 'Well, anyway—it's been a long day and I expect we're both tired.'

'Yes,' she said. She'd had as much as she could stand for the moment, and she guessed he felt the same.

They climbed into opposite sides of the bed, solemnly bid each other goodnight and turned out the lights. Almost at once Holly discovered that she really was worn out, and when she closed her eyes she was asleep in seconds.

She awoke because a strange noise was reaching out through her sleep, seeking her, imploring her attention. As soon as she opened her eyes she realised what had disturbed her. A low growl, almost like a moan, was coming from the other side of the bed.

Matteo was lying on his front, his face turned towards her, half-buried in the pillow. One hand also lay on his pillow, clenching and unclenching as choking sounds came from him. He was talking in a language that Holly didn't understand.

'Matteo,' she said softly. 'Are you all right?'

The reply was a torrent of unintelligible words, while his hand clenched convulsively. Only then did she realise that he was still asleep.

'Matteo,' she repeated, uncertain whether to awaken him or not. The feeling of pain that came from him was too intense to be ignored.

His voice changed, becoming sharp. 'No,' he said. 'No— no—no—'

Then he gave a sudden, convulsive movement and threw himself over onto his back. He was breathing harshly now while, 'No—no—no...' poured from his mouth.

Acting instinctively, Holly seized his hand, holding it between hers until its jerky movements subsided. At the same time the heaving of his chest became less violent.

'It's all right,' she told him softly. 'I'm here—I'm here.'

Now he lay still. The only sign of his recent disturbance was the frown creasing his brow.

'I'm here,' she repeated. 'It's going to be all right.'

Slowly the frown faded and he seemed to breathe more easily, but his hand did not release hers. Holly eased herself down in the bed, trying not to disturb him.

She had embarked on this strange marriage with little idea of what might be facing her, but telling herself that she was ready for anything. Now she wondered if she had been too rash. He depended on her for something that might be beyond her power.

Too late now. She had made promises that bound her as irrevocably as the fingers clasped around hers, while he sank back into peaceful sleep, growing still. After a long time he released her, and she was able to draw her hand away. Then she stayed as she was, watching him, motionless, until she too fell asleep.

She awoke again later to find herself sitting up, unable to remember how it had happened, but instantly alert. She must have slept for hours because the room was filled with a soft, dim light that told her dawn was breaking. Cautiously she turned her head to where he slept.

Once again he'd taken her by surprise. After the disturbance of the night she'd imagined him sleeping curled up in a defensive position, his arms a barrier against a world that had betrayed him. Instead he lay on his back, his arms flung wide, his jacket open, revealing a chest that was thick with dark, curly hair, abandoned, unprotected.

In what other way was he different from how she had imagined? How many sides did he have, and would he live long enough for her to find out?

That was the reality, she reminded herself: he might die at any moment. She closed her eyes, trying to resist the anguish that shivered through her, but it wouldn't be denied. Somehow, while she thought she was fighting him off, he'd secured a grip on her heart.

She'd told him once that her weakness was a longing to be needed, but that was when she'd seen him as too strong to need anyone. Her real feelings had pounced on her like a tiger leaping from the darkness, overwhelming her before she realised.

The width of the bed should have been a protection. But one of his arms reached across the space between, the fingertips temptingly close. And there was no protection from the thoughts that crowded in on her. The one that hounded her most was the one kiss they'd shared on the night when the barriers began to come down, and he'd later revealed the truth about his torment.

They'd hastily replaced the barriers, but there was no way to blot out the memory of a kiss so fierce and thrilling that they'd both backed off, eyes wary, hearts in denial.

The moment had briefly glittered tonight as they talked, and she'd shut it away hastily. But in the dark warmth it had returned, taking advantage of her defenceless sleep to remind her how his body felt, pressed against hers. In just a few blazing moments he seemed to have imprinted himself on her so that he was still there, his lips touching her mouth, his hand firm in the small of her back.

That hand looked different now, relaxed, gentle. His face, too, was softer than she had ever seen it, although dark with a night's growth of beard. His frown was gone, but she could see that the tensions of his life had not completely vanished. Beneath the surface peace was a wariness, as though life on the verge of disaster was the only kind possible for him.

While she was wondering if she should awaken him, Matteo opened his eyes and looked directly into hers. He didn't move, but she had the feeling that a quietness had settled over him, as though he'd found what he wanted, and was glad.

'Have you been there all the time?' he whispered.

She nodded.

'Yes, of course—stupid of me—'

'Not stupid,' she said. 'We aren't used to this.'

'Thank you for being there.'

So he knew, she thought. He might not remember exactly, but somewhere, deep inside, he'd sensed her in the night, holding on to him.

His lips moved, speaking her name silently, and he reached up to touch her face, trailing his fingertips gently down her cheek. He looked almost puzzled, as though trying to understand how this had come about. When his hand settled behind her head she hesitated only a moment before leaning slowly down. She could feel him trembling and knew that he must be able to sense the same in her. This wasn't wise but it was inevitable. She couldn't sleep beside him all night and remain cool.

She moved slightly so that his free hand could drift naturally across her breast, and braced herself for the sweet sensation.

There was a knock at the door.

Then Liza's voice called, 'Can I come in?'

Matteo closed his eyes and a shudder went through him. Holly took a deep breath, forcing herself to be calm.

'Yes,' she called brightly. 'You can come in.'

Instinctively she tried to draw away from him, thinking only of calming the tingling in her body. But he held her, murmuring, 'Remember what we said? Neutered cats.'

She could have screamed at the intrusion of the homely into what promised to be magic. But he was right. So she let him draw her down so that her head fell on his shoulder, and draped an arm around his neck, just managing to settle before the door opened and Liza came in.

She beamed at what she saw, then went back outside and returned pushing a light trolley.

'I brought your coffee,' she said.

Somehow they managed to say the right words, pulling themselves up in bed, smiling and acting as though nothing could give them greater pleasure. Which, in one sense, was true, Holly thought. This was all for Liza. Remember that.

But it was hard to stick to her resolutions when she was trembling with sweet urgency as never before. Whatever

Matteo had promised about keeping his distance, in another moment he would have cast virtue and honour to the winds, and made love to her with her full consent.

She took her consolation in the knowledge that the vital moment was a success. Liza's world seemed to have tilted in the way she needed, which meant that the arrangement was working.

And there was always tonight, she thought, feeling happiness creep through her. She tried to communicate that thought to Matteo, but he seemed anxious to get back to his own room, almost unable to meet her eyes.

That night his clerk called to say that the judge was working very late. By the time he arrived home she was asleep.

Two days later Galina returned to her own home. She never spoke of the dangerous subject again, but she smiled at Holly in a way that conveyed her meaning unmistakably.

Matteo travelled everywhere with a police escort, leaving early in the morning and arriving home late. Then he would spend his time with Liza, leaving little time for Holly.

Gradually she realised that her first suspicion was correct. He was avoiding her. Now he slept in his own room, with an alarm set for the early hours so that he could join her then, slipping in on the far side and staying there. Clearly the danger that had almost engulfed them once was not to be allowed to happen again.

In her odd moments alone, Holly watched the news compulsively. One evening there was a brief snippet about Fortese. She'd seen his face before, but only in newspapers that she had hastily put aside to keep them from Liza. Now she had the chance to consider him properly.

He might be a villain but he didn't have the face of a thug. His features were narrow, gentlemanly, and all the more chilling for that. Eyes like ice, the smile of a dead man. He had committed several murders and always escaped by bribing or frightening witnesses or the judge.

But in Matteo he had met his match. On Matteo's orders the witnesses received double the usual protection and, although clearly scared, they had given their damn-ing testimony.

Matteo could be neither bribed nor bullied. He had imposed a sentence of thirty years. Fortese had listened, motionless, to the sentence. Then, at the very last moment, he had spoken.

'No prison can hold me,' he said. 'I shall find you and kill you.'

Commotion. The police pounced and hustled him out. Judge Fallucci showed no expression as he collected his things and departed.

Watching it now, Holly felt a chill of fear consume her. Matteo could take as many precautions as he liked. Fortese would win. That was the message.

That night she undressed thoughtfully, switched out the light and sat up in bed, her arms wrapped around her knees, staring into the distance.

On the other side of the door she could hear Matteo moving around. She listened, tense, wondering if he would come in, but, as she had expected, he made no move towards her. After a while the light under the door went out.

She waited, coming to a decision. It took all her courage, but she wouldn't turn back now. She didn't know how much time there might be left.

At the door she raised her hand to knock, then lowered it. He was her husband, and she was blowed if she was going to knock. She tried the door and, to her relief, it was not locked.

Like so many other things about him, the room surprised her. It was small, almost monastic. In the corner was a narrow bed, on which he sat, his elbows on his knees, his hands clasped, his forehead drooped wearily against them.

He was too lost in his own thoughts to hear her enter, and didn't know she was there until she dropped down on her knees beside him.

'I'm sorry if I disturbed you,' he said.

'Why, because you're afraid you might have to talk to me?' she asked, looking up seriously into his face.

'No, I just...' but he gave up at once, confronted by the truth in her eyes.

'I needed to talk to you tonight,' she said. 'There was a programme going back over your history with Fortese—'

'Did Liza—?'

'No, she knows nothing except that you're unusually busy just now, but she doesn't know why. We talk all the time, except when the physiotherapist comes to work with her leg, or a teacher comes to give her a lesson.

'When I can be alone I read the papers or watch the news, and there are so many things I want to ask you, but you hide away.'

'There's nothing for you to worry about.'

'Don't patronise me, Matteo,' she said, suddenly angry. 'I'm not a fool. I know exactly what there is to worry about. Every day I listen for you to come home, knowing that one day you may not come. I tell myself that if it was bad news someone would telephone first, and if there's no phone call then you're on your way. I try so hard to believe that.

'When you enter the house I want to run and see you, to touch you and make sure that you're real, but I keep back and let Liza have you to herself. I have to be content with staying in the shadows, but I thought we'd have more than that. The first night—'

'The first night I came close to breaking my solemn word to you—'

'Be damned to your word!' she said, so fiercely that he stared. 'Stop being a lawyer all the time. All right, you promised to keep your distance but you didn't swear an oath about it in court. That kind of foolish promise is made to be broken. What kind of man *can* keep such a promise with a woman he wants?'

'Who says I want you?' he demanded in a voice that was as brutal as he could make it. Much more of this and he would go mad.

But nothing worked with this woman. Instead of being dumbfounded she flung back, *'You do!'* in a voice of pure rage. 'You tell me every moment, and you tell me most when you're trying hardest not to. You want me as much as I want you, so for pity's sake give up the pretence.'

She was still kneeling beside him, her face upturned, the moonlight shadowing the hollows of her breast. Moisture gleamed on his forehead as he seized her shoulders in cruel fingers.

'Will you stop this?' he demanded. 'I'm trying to act like a man of honour.'

'Then be damned to your honour too. Forget it. If Fortese shoots you down, shall I engrave that on your tomb? Here lies a man of honour. He kept his word to the end, but he left his wife alone and desolate, with an empty heart.'

She drew a deep breath and took a calculated risk. 'Unless, of course, honour is just another word for fear.'

'Are you mad?' he flashed at her. 'Of course it's fear. How can I not be afraid? Yes, I want you. I've wanted you for a long time, and that first night I nearly took you. But I'm glad I didn't because where can it end? We've grown closer than we meant to, you know that. But who am I to dare to get close to a woman? To dare to l—'

'To love?' she challenged him. 'Say it.'

But he shook his head.

'At any other time I'd reach out to you,' he growled, 'and stop at nothing until I'd made you mine. I'd fight anyone, even you, to make you love me. I'd take you to bed and love you until you forgot the whole world, and I'd enclose your heart in mine so that we were one—if only—'

He sighed heavily.

'If only...'

She tried to answer but something was making her throat ache.

'But what right do I have to try to win your love when I probably won't be here much longer? We have to be realistic. Fortese specialises in murder. He's practically a genius, and he'll probably get to me.'

'Don't—' she whispered in agony.

'I must. One day—when this is over—if we get through it—'

'We will. You're not going to die,' she said frantically.

'I pray to God I won't, now that I have so much to live for. But I won't risk leaving you when our love has only just started—'

'You fool!' she said violently. 'Don't you know it's already too late for that? Do you think our love hasn't started just because we haven't been to bed? Do you think the love of the heart somehow doesn't count if the body hasn't loved too?'

'How do you come to know so much about love,' he whispered, 'when I know so little?'

'Enough,' she said, laying her lips against his. 'No more. *Basta!*'

She had made her decision and now there must be an end to this. She only wanted him.

It was her kiss rather than his, but he gave himself to it with a whole heart, like a man who had suddenly discovered the elusive answer. He moved gently at first, exploring her lips with his own, then claiming her more deeply.

Slowly he rose, drawing her to her feet so that he could more easily remove her nightgown. His own clothes followed quickly, and she knew her own cautious moment. She was being asked to give so much trust, and for her, as for him, total trust was the last great barrier. But he seemed to understand that, drawing her gently down onto the bed with him.

'You're right,' he growled. 'It's too late to back away.'

'I don't want to back away. Haven't you understood anything?'

Once she'd said that, it really was too late. At first he made love to her slowly, with a restraint through which she could still sense a thrilling urgency. And when he saw her smiling at him in dreamy delight he made love to her again, but without restraint now, so that she too could throw off the world and exist only for him.

When they lay in each other's arms later she gave a slight shiver as the world returned.

'Summer's over,' he said. 'Now it's getting cold at night. We should get warm again before you catch pneumonia. Let's go back to your room. The bed's bigger.'

'No,' she pleaded, holding on to him. 'I don't want it to be over yet.'

He nodded, catching her meaning at once. This narrow, uncomfortable little bed was the place where love had reached its first fulfilment, and they were reluctant to leave it. The grandest bed in the world could not compare.

'Let's put something on and go under the covers, then,' he said, rescuing their clothes from the floor. Safely back in bed, they drew up sheets and blankets. There was so little room that they had to huddle together, lest one of them fall out, but they didn't mind that.

'I can never be sorry,' he whispered after a while. 'But—'

'No,' she said, laying her fingers over his mouth. 'No buts. I forbid it.'

'Going to be a bullying wife, huh?'

'If you force me.'

'You're so reckless that I admire you for it, even while it scares me. Suppose I die and leave you with a child? Have you thought of that?'

'You talk of me having a baby as though it were the worst thing that could happen, but it wouldn't be. At least I'd have part of you left.'

'Where do you get your courage from?' he asked tenderly.

'From you.'

'And if I'm no longer there?'

'The same answer. I'll still get my courage from you. You'll always be there, with me. But don't talk of that. I'm not going to be gloomy tonight. There's too much to be happy about. You're not going to die.'

'My darling—'

'You're not. I won't allow it. Do you think *he* is stronger than me?'

'Nobody is stronger than you,' he said fervently.

Dreams. Fantasies. The real world was still out there, still deadly. But she would fight it. She let her thoughts range free, seeking something light to bear her up, and at last a soft choke of laughter broke from her.

'What is it?' he asked, almost alarmed. 'What the devil is funny about this?'

'To think I accused you of always shouting. It was me doing the shouting this time. I had to or you wouldn't have listened. I'll remember that in future. Shout your husband down. If he won't shut up, at least you'll make a great noise together.'

Laughter welled up inside him, threatening to break out in a roar that would wake the house. Instead he buried his face against her in an agony of bittersweet joy, and laughed and laughed until he wept.

As the morning light grew, Liza came along the corridor and slipped noiselessly into Holly's room. Finding nobody there, she went to the inner door and opened it cautiously.

Looking around the edge, she saw the narrow bed, and the two who lay there sleeping, arms wrapped about each other in perfect contentment.

She crept away, smiling to herself.

CHAPTER TWELVE

NOTHING in Holly's life recently had been what she would have once called normal, so the strangeness of the next few weeks was merely another kind of unreality.

It had its own intense sweetness. The closeness she shared with Matteo was past naming. It might have been love, but they never spoke the word, by night or day. When there were others around they maintained a friendly demeanour, full of propriety but no passion. At night they would go wordlessly into each other's arms, sharing the joy of mutual need and fulfilment. Afterwards they would sink into the sleep of the blessed.

But hanging over this was the ever-present danger. Time passed without the police tracking down their quarry. He was nowhere. He was everywhere.

She would see Matteo off in the morning knowing that she might never see him again, and welcome him home in the evening, knowing that it might be for the last time.

The house was under permanent guard, although for Liza's sake the men didn't wear uniforms, and could have been gardeners. When the time came for her to go to school Matteo hired tutors so that she needed not leave the house. Between her lessons, visits from the physiotherapist and her time with Holly, she was content.

Her condition was improving, although she still had to take a nap in the afternoons. Often she argued, but Holly would hold firm, except for once when she allowed the child to stay up and finish a book that had seized her imagination. But the next day Liza seemed sleepy, and made no protest about going to bed for an hour.

Holly took the chance of a nap herself. She had had almost no sleep the night before.

She awoke to find Anna shaking her.

'The little girl isn't well,' she said anxiously. 'She's just been sick.'

She raced into Liza's room and found her sitting up, being comforted by a maid, who'd removed the soiled dress. The child was weeping.

'Hello, darling,' Holly said as cheerfully as possible. 'Let's see what's wrong with you.'

'My head aches,' Liza complained.

Gently Holly laid her hand on her forehead, startled by what she found there. Liza's temperature had climbed to an alarming height, and she was trying to cover her eyes.

'*Piccina*, look at me,' Holly urged.

'No, my eyes hurt,' Liza choked.

'All right, don't worry,' she said. 'Everything is going to be all right.'

Outside the door she spoke urgently to Anna. 'I need the family doctor. Please call him and tell him to come quickly.'

The doctor, an elderly man who had treated the family for years, was there in half an hour. He looked grave as he took Liza's temperature and looked at her flushed, tearful face.

When they'd left the room Holly said, 'A friend of my mother had a child who suffered like this. It was meningitis.'

'That's what I think, too. She must go to hospital at once. I'll arrange the ambulance to take her to San Piero.'

He made the call while Holly went out to find one of the police guards and explain the situation. The man looked worried.

'Is it really necessary to move her?' he asked.

'It wouldn't be safe not to,' Holly told him tensely.

Matteo had left her with a special phone number for the court, to be used only in emergencies. There was still an hour left before the sitting ended for the day. She dialled the number and spoke to Matteo's clerk.

'Please tell him that his daughter is seriously ill with possible meningitis, and has been taken to San Piero,' she said tersely.

The ambulance was there fast, and within a few minutes they were on the road, streaming along the Appian Way to Rome. Holly stayed beside Liza, trying to hold her attention, but not succeeding. The little girl's eyes were glazed, her breath came in gasps, and although she seemed to look directly at Holly it was plain that she didn't know she was there.

'Hold on, darling,' Holly urged. 'Just a little further. And Poppa...'

She was going to say that Poppa would be with them soon, but suddenly the words wouldn't come. Would he really stop work for this child who had lost her place in his heart? The answer should be, Of course he would, but, to her horror, she realised that she wasn't sure.

It made no difference, she realised. Liza was beyond hearing. If her father was to let her down now, she might never even know.

'No,' Holly said frantically. 'Darling, wake up. It's going to be all right.'

But the only answer was Liza's harsh breathing.

'He'll be at the hospital,' Holly assured herself. 'He hasn't so far to travel. He'll get there before us.'

To her relief they were turning through the main gates of the hospital. The ambulance rear doors swung open and she hastened to move out of the way of the nurses. In moments Liza was on a trolley being wheeled inside.

There was no sign of Matteo in Reception and when she asked at the desk, nobody had seen him.

Then she had no time to think of anything but Liza as she was whisked away for tests by grave-faced medical staff. A nurse asked for details.

'She was fine this morning,' Holly said wretchedly. 'A little less lively than usual but I thought she'd missed out on sleep. If only—'

'It comes on very swiftly,' the nurse said. 'Often there's nothing to warn anyone until the last moment.'

'She had a nap and when she woke up she was sick… her head hurt.'

'Her father—'

'I've left a message for him.'

But why isn't he here? she thought. It doesn't take so long to get here from the court, if he left at once.

If he left at once.

But did he? Did he remember that she was not his child, and so bring the blank down over his feelings? Did he wait until the last minute, calling it his duty?

At the thought, a desolate wind seemed to sweep over her heart. In the short, precious time allowed them they had discovered so much happiness that it was painful to think of the little girl kept on the outside. Sometimes she had a wretched feeling that if Matteo couldn't learn to accept Liza completely, then her own love for him would always remain incomplete, and perhaps would not last.

But he would be here any moment. She was sure of it.

Things began to move quickly. The doctor, who knew Liza from her last time in the hospital, confronted Holly with the final diagnosis.

'Bacterial meningitis,' he said with quiet gravity. 'Which, I'm afraid, means that it's very bad. I'm going to put her on intravenous injections of antibiotics to combat the infection. You too will need antibiotics in case you have contracted it from her, also her father.'

There was a question in his voice and Holly was forced to say, 'He will be here soon. I sent a message.'

'I hope you stressed the urgency because...' he hesitated before saying slowly, 'things could turn very bleak indeed, very soon.'

She nodded, sick at heart.

Matteo would not be here—at least, not in time. Liza would die without the comfort of his love, and her own love for him would wither away.

But she couldn't think too much about that now. Whatever misery might wait in the future, only Liza mattered at this moment.

When she was allowed to see her again she found the little girl lying still, attached to machines, her face dangerously flushed. Holly touched her hand lightly, but there was no response.

Would there ever be one? Holly wondered. Or would she die without knowing that her father had finally turned his back on her?

She settled beside the bed, the child's hand in hers, and waited in patient silence, while her heart began to harden.

The nurse stayed in the room, checking machines regularly, but Holly was aware of nothing but herself and Liza. It was as though they were both travelling down a dark tunnel that led to the unknown, with only each other for comfort. And there was nobody else with them.

Once she felt Liza's hand move gently in hers, and her lips framed a word that might have been 'Poppa'. But Holly couldn't be sure.

Lost in this unhappy dream, she barely heard the footsteps outside. But as they grew closer she became aware of a commotion, voices raised in protest. As she looked up the door was flung open and Matteo burst in. His eyes were wild and he blurted out fierce questions as though they terrified him.

'How is she? What's happened?'

'She has bacterial meningitis, and she's very bad. Why didn't you come before? I called hours ago.'

'I know that now, but I didn't get the message at the time. I'll tell you all about it later. *Tell me she isn't dying.*'

'I can't,' Holly said softly, moving back to let him come to the bed.

It was too much to take in quickly, but one thing reached her: he hadn't ignored her message. He was still the man she believed in.

He sat down, taking Liza's hand, speaking to her urgently.

'She can't hear you, I'm afraid,' the nurse said. 'She's deeply unconscious.'

'She's so hot,' Matteo murmured. 'How did it all happen?'

Holly told him the day's events, but she could tell that he barely heard. All his attention was for the little girl on the bed, her hand resting unresponsively in his.

'*Piccina,*' he said urgently, 'wake up, please. I'm here. Poppa's here.'

'No,' came a faint whisper from the bed. 'He won't come.'

Matteo and Holly looked quickly at each other.

'What did she say?' he demanded breathlessly. 'I didn't catch it.'

'She said her father won't come,' Holly told him reluctantly.

'But I'm here,' he said frantically. '*Piccina,* Poppa is here.'

'No—won't come—he didn't come—for ages and ages—I cried for him but he didn't come.'

'What does she mean by that?' he demanded.

She could only shake her head, desperate at her failure to help him. Her mind seemed to have seized up. He was looking at her out of anguished eyes.

'He didn't come,' Liza murmured again.

'What can I do?' he begged. '*Holly, for pity's sake, help me.*'

'I can't, I—'

'He didn't come,' came the feeble croak, 'he didn't even come to see us off...'

Holly's head shot up as the answer came to her with the dazzling clarity of light. She could see them, a woman and a child sitting in a garden, beside a monument, the child pouring out things she'd never told before, because there was nobody to tell.

'She's talking about that other time,' she breathed, 'just before last Christmas, when she went away with her mother and you didn't go to the station to see them off. She knew something was wrong because that had never happened before. She's living back then.'

'But can't she tell that I'm here now?'

In her agitation Holly shook her head violently.

'Nothing's happening *now,* don't you see? Now doesn't exist. She's gone back to the time life stopped for her. When the train turned over she was caught in her mother's arms. Carol became unconscious but Liza stayed awake. She was alone and frightened and she wanted you, but you didn't come.'

'I knew nothing about it. Dear God!' Matteo dropped his

head down onto the bed. After a moment he raised it. 'What can I say to her?'

'I can't tell you that,' Holly said. 'But it must come from your heart, or she'll know.'

'Poppa—Poppa…' Liza's voice had risen onto a note of anguish. 'Where are you?'

'I'm here, *piccina*.' He took both her hands in his, searching her face, trying to will her to open her eyes.

'No—no—you never came—Mamma said—I didn't belong to you…'

He grew very still then, his eyes fixed on the little girl in a kind of dread.

'Carol couldn't have told her that,' he murmured. 'She couldn't—'

'I'm afraid she must have,' Holly said.

'But how could she do anything so cruel? How could anyone…? Then she knows everything. Oh, God!'

'No, I don't think she does,' Holly said suddenly. 'Children put their own meanings on things. She won't understand that phrase as we understand it.'

He closed his eyes. 'Please let her wake up. I have to explain to her.'

'How will you explain this?'

'I don't know.'

The nurse brought another chair and they sat on each side of the bed. Holly reached out her hand to him, he took it but his eyes remained fixed on the little girl on the bed, breathing uneasily.

'Liza,' he said urgently, 'Liza!'

There was no reply.

'No,' he said in a low voice, 'no, no! *Please, not now*!'

Holly watched him through her tears, feeling his agony that

he had learned the truth of his own heart when it might already be too late.

Silence and darkness. Time passed. It felt like a lifetime but the clock showed that it was only an hour.

Silence, deep and unfathomable.

'I was afraid you weren't coming,' Holly said quietly.

'I suppose I deserved that, but you might have trusted me a little more. No—' he stopped himself quickly '—I don't mean that. Why should you trust me about this? What have I done to deserve trust?'

'It isn't your fault—'

'Not this time, but other times—you thought I'd leave her lying here ill? But I wouldn't. I couldn't get here sooner because I was held up by Fortese. He got into the courtroom and held us all at gunpoint.'

'Oh, dear God—'

'It's all right. It's over. He was too clever for his own good. He insisted on making a speech, saying exactly why he hated me, and that gave the guards time to break in. They grabbed him before he could fire, and hauled him back to gaol. He's back behind bars right now.'

'You mean,' she breathed, hardly daring to hope, 'it's over?'

'Yes,' he said quietly. 'Yes, it is.'

She should be filled with happiness, but the joy was muted by the knowledge of tragedy still threatening. The child on the bed lay motionless as they sat on either side of her. Matteo spoke her name again, but there was no response.

'It was this way once before,' he said suddenly.

'How do you mean?'

'The night we married I had a bad dream, but you drove it away. I can't remember details now, but I can still hear your voice saying, "I'm here, I'm here."'

'I didn't know if you'd heard me.'

'I think your voice could find me through anything. Tell me your secret because I need it desperately now. How do I reach out to my daughter?'

The words 'my daughter' caused a small well-spring of happiness to start in her.

'You just did,' she said.

Liza stirred and took a long breath.

'*Piccina*!' Matteo was beside her at once, taking both her hands back into his. 'I'm here—I'm here…'

Consciously or unconsciously he was echoing the words Holly had spoken to him on their wedding night, words that shaped themselves into a promise of comfort and fidelity forever. But could that promise work again?

'I'm here—'

'Why—didn't you come?' she cried fretfully, her eyes still closed. 'Mamma said—I don't belong to you.'

He looked up at Holly. 'But what does she understand by that?'

Suddenly it came to her, the inspiration she wanted, the only thing that could help him now.

'*Piccina*,' she said, turning to Liza, 'your parents were both very jealous about you. They each loved you so much that they wanted you just for themselves.'

He drew a sharp breath as understanding came. It was as though a light had come on inside him. He leaned closer to Liza and began to speak in a kind of imploring voice.

'Mamma said you were hers and I said you were mine— all mine, because I didn't want to share you. We became angry, and that's why she took you away, and told you that you didn't belong to me, only to her.'

'But I do—belong to you?'

'Yes, *piccina*, you're all mine—'

'Always—'

'Always and forever.'

Suddenly Liza took a long breath. A long, agonising silence, then she opened her eyes to see Matteo there.

'Hello Poppa,' she whispered.

'Hello,' he said shakily, dropping his forehead onto their entwined hands, while his shoulders shook.

After a moment he looked up, this time at Holly, and spoke through his tears.

'Hello,' he said.

As soon as Liza was out of danger Matteo arranged for her to come home. Her room was turned into a mini-hospital, and three nurses were hired to give her round-the-clock care.

He spent as much time with her as possible, insisting on taking time off from work, relishing his happiness, and safe-guarding it.

Holly would have stood back, letting them be alone to discover each other again. But neither of them would allow that. They opened their arms, drawing her into their magic circle.

Alone with Matteo, the magic was different, profound, breathtaking. Now he could speak openly about his love, but it was when he said nothing at all that she knew it most deeply. Since the day she had drawn him back from the precipice he had placed himself in her hands entirely.

Soon it would be Christmas, the first that the three of them would share. As the weather grew colder and the leaves fell from the trees Holly found herself haunted by a strange thought. She was unsure about confiding it to Matteo. His heart had opened further than she had dared to hope, but was even his generosity enough for this last step?

One day as they sat together he gave her a sudden, curious look, and asked, 'What are you thinking?'

'I just had an odd idea…'

'Share it with me.'

'You may not like it.'

He smiled. 'But I shall trust it.'

'All right. I was thinking that the person I feel most sorry for is Alec Martin.'

'Carol's lover? The man who took my daughter.'

'Yes, but—'

'But he didn't take my daughter,' he said, reading her mind as he could do so easily now. 'I took his, didn't I?'

'You've had her all her life. She met him only once, on the train, and she didn't like him.'

He nodded, beginning to understand.

'Carol did him a wrong, just as she did me—perhaps more so. All that time he had a lovely little daughter, and he didn't know.'

'It's you she loves,' Holly said.

'Yes, and me she snuggles against and kisses goodnight. I thought he'd taken everything away from me, but actually it was the other way around.'

He walked slowly out into the garden, and this time she made no effort to go with him. He needed time to clarify his own thoughts. She had given him the lead, but the conclusion must be his own.

He didn't mention it again for two days, but then he said, 'I need to go out. Will you come with me?'

In the car he explained, 'It took me a while to check out where he was buried, but I've found him now. I was afraid that they might have taken him back to England, but it seems that he had no close family to care.'

The cemetery was small and bleak, a place for people whom nobody wanted. Here were no beautiful monuments, only small, ugly slabs that almost seemed to shrink with the cold. At last they found Alec Martin's, with his name and dates.

'He was only thirty-three when he died,' Matteo said. 'And his whole adult life had been taken up making enough money to claim his family back from me. Now he has nothing.

'I've hated him, but I never before wondered how much he must have hated me.'

He was silent for a moment before looking at the grave and speaking, almost as though there were someone there who could hear.

'I came here today...' He hesitated, and for a moment Holly thought he would be unable to go on. But then he lifted his head. 'I came to say thank you for our daughter, and to promise you that I'll always look after her.'

His face softened. 'You have my word on that.'

He drew Holly's hand through his arm and led her away from the loneliness. The air was cold with frost and dusk was falling, but through the trees they could see lights, beckoning them on to another place, where there was warmth, hope and new life.

Just before they reached the lights he stopped and said, 'But for you, I could never have understood. I could never even have made a beginning.'

'The beginning will go on,' she promised.

'Only if you're with me.'

'I will be—always.'

He kissed her tenderly.

'Let's go home,' he said.

* * * * *

Gwen took a taxi to the Yellow Parrot, and with each passing block she grew more tense. It didn't take a rocket scientist to figure out that this dive was in the worst part of town. Gwen had learned to take care of herself, but the minute she entered the bar, she realized that a smart woman would have brought a gun with her. The interior was hot, smelly and dirty, and the air was so smoky that it looked as if a pea soup fog had settled inside the building. Before she had gone three feet, an old drunk came up to her and asked for money. Sidestepping him, she searched for someone who looked as if he or she might actually work here, someone other than the prostitutes who were trolling for customers.

After fending off a couple of grasping young men and ignoring several vulgar propositions in an odd mixture of Spanish and English, Gwen found the bar. She ordered a beer from the burly, bearded bartender. When he set the beer in front of her, she took the opportunity to speak to him.

"I'm looking for a man. An older American man, in his seventies. He was probably with a younger woman. This man is my father and—"

"*No hablo inglés.*"

"Oh." He didn't speak English and she didn't speak Spanish. Now what?

While she was considering her options, Gwen noticed a young man in skintight black pants and an open black shirt, easing closer and closer to her as he made his way past the other men at the bar.

Great. That was all she needed—some horny young guy mistaking her for a prostitute.

"*Señorita.*" His voice was softly accented and slightly slurred. His breath smelled of liquor. "You are all alone, *sí?*"

"Please, go away," Gwen said. "I'm not interested."

He laughed, as if he found her attitude amusing. "Then it is for me to make you interested. I am Marco. And you are…?"

"Leaving," Gwen said.

She realized it had been a mistake to come here alone tonight. Any effort to unearth information about her father in a place like this was probably pointless. She would do better to come back tomorrow and try to speak to the owner. But when she tried to move past her ardent young suitor, he reached out and grabbed her arm. She tensed.

Looking him right in the eyes, she told him, "Let go of me. Right now."

"But you cannot leave. The night is young."

Gwen tugged on her arm, trying to break free. He tightened his hold, his fingers biting into her flesh. With her heart beating rapidly as her basic fight-or-flight instinct kicked in, she glared at the man.

"I'm going to ask you one more time to let me go."

Grinning smugly, he grabbed her other arm, holding her in place.

Suddenly, seemingly from out of nowhere, a big hand clamped down on Marco's shoulder, jerked him back and spun him around. Suddenly free, Gwen swayed slightly but managed to retain her balance as she watched in amazement as a tall, lanky man in jeans and cowboy boots shoved her would-be suitor up against the bar.

"I believe the lady asked you real nice to let her go," the man said, in a deep Texas drawl. "Where I come from, a gentleman respects a lady's wishes."

Marco grumbled something unintelligible in Spanish. Probably cursing, Gwen thought. Or maybe praying. If she were Marco, she would be praying that the big, rugged American wouldn't beat her to a pulp.

Apparently Marco was not as smart as she was. When the Texan released him, he came at her rescuer, obviously intending to fight him. The Texan took Marco out with two swift punches, sending the younger man to the floor. Gwen glanced down at where Marco lay sprawled flat on his back, unconscious.

Her hero turned to her. "Ma'am, are you all right?"

She nodded. The man was about six-two, with a sunburned tan, sun-streaked brown hair and azure-blue eyes.

"What's a lady like you doing in a place like this?" he asked.

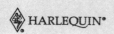

EVERLASTING LOVE™

Every great love has a story to tell ™

Save $1.⁰⁰ off

**the purchase of
any Harlequin
Everlasting Love novel**

Coupon valid from January 1, 2007
until April 30, 2007.

Valid at retail outlets in the U.S. only.
Limit one coupon per customer.

5 65373 00076 2   (8100)0 11302

HEUSCPN0407

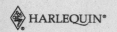
HARLEQUIN®

EVERLASTING LOVE™

Every great love has a story to tell™

Fall from Grace

Kristi Gold

Save $1.⁰⁰ off

the purchase of any Harlequin Everlasting Love novel

Coupon valid from January 1, 2007 until April 30, 2007.

Valid at retail outlets in Canada only. Limit one coupon per customer.

RETAILER: Harlequin Enterprises Limited will pay the face value of this coupon plus 10.25¢ if submitted by the customer for this product only. Any other use constitutes fraud. Coupon is nonassignable. Void if taxed, prohibited or restricted by law. Consumer must pay any government taxes. Void if copied. Nielsen Clearing House customers submit coupons and proof of sales to: Harlequin Enterprises Ltd. P.O. Box 3000, Saint John, N.B. E2L 4L3. Non–NCH retailer—for reimbursement submit coupons and proof of sales directly to: Harlequin Enterprises Ltd., Retail Marketing Department, 225 Duncan Mill Rd., Don Mills, Ontario M3B 3K9, Canada. Valid in Canada only. ® is a trademark of Harlequin Enterprises Ltd. Trademarks marked with ® are registered in the United States and/or other countries.

52607370

HECDNCPN0407

This February...

Catch NASCAR Superstar *Carl Edwards* in
SPEED DATING!

Kendall assesses risk for a living—so she's the last person you'd expect to see on the arm of a race-car driver who thrives on the unpredictable. But when a bizarre turn of events—and NASCAR hotshot Dylan Hargreave—inspire her to trade in her ever-so-structured existence for "life in the fast lane" she starts to feel she might be on to something!

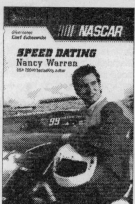

Coming Next Month